# MARATHON

Constantine & Basil Vassilaros

*This book is dedicated to all marathon runners and history enthusiasts.*

# CONTENTS

# PREFACE

*— The following is an account of the author, Constantine Vassilaros.*

Marathon!

If you were to ask any long-distance runner what this is, they are likely to tell you it is a 'prestigious race across a vast distance where one's endurance and determination is tested'.

Around the world, there is at least one Marathon Race. Within the USA, I am aware of two of them—the New York Marathon and the Boston Marathon, and I am sure there are plenty more. Here, in South Africa, the most well-known race is the Comrades Marathon—an annual race between the two cities of Durban and Pietermaritzburg.

Personally, I never thought much of running long distances. In my youth, I could run all day kicking a soccer ball, yet if asked to run more than five kilometres…well, it would be an anathema to me. However, fate led me to become involved in the sport, which changed my attitude.

In the mid-70s, a close friend and colleague, Brian G., took to the sport and began participating in five to ten kilometre runs. Soon after, he attempted even longer distances, such as the Richmond Run. In order to do so, he required a Second—someone to drive to checkpoints and ensure he remained hydrated and safe. He asked if I was interested, and I agreed (mostly out of curiosity and to be honest, I enjoyed it).

So, I became his official Second.

He ran several races, including the Muden Race, where afterwards I received two bottles of orange wine and a beautiful breakfast, courtesy of the Muden Running Club. A year later, Brian decided to run the Comrades Marathon and I was eager to help him in the race ahead, where I would witness the drama that usually unfolds in such renowned runs.

After running his qualifying race, and a month before the big one, he ran from Pietermaritzburg to Hillcrest, to familiarize himself with the route.

On the morning of the Comrades, at four o'clock, we arrived at the starting ground in Pietermaritzburg. I parked the car in market square and we walked to the starting line by the city hall, where Brian went to confirm his registration while I mingled with the other runners, their Seconds, and race officials.

With half and hour to go, I found the perfect spot in front of the two-metre-high temporary stage near the city hall, where the dignitaries stood, to watch the race. From there, I had a clear view of the starting line, not twenty metres away, where the runners warmed up. A buzz of excitement filled the air, spectators searched for their own places and officials took their positions—all eagerly awaiting the race.

Finally, the city hall's Big Ben look-alike clock tower rang its bell. At the end of its last stoke I heard someone above me crowing like a rooster. I looked up to see an old man among the officials crowing while making funny faces. Initially, I thought the man either hadn't recovered from the previous night's drinking, or he escaped from Fort Napier Asylum. If so, how did he even get up there!? It was sometime later, I was informed that I was privileged to witness Mr. Max Trimborn performing his famous rooster crow— which up until today, a recording is used at the start of every Comrades Marathon.

Once Mr. Trimborn finished, the gun fired and a stampede for the lead commenced, as those ahead sprinted off while the back eased to a walking pace. So far, the race appeared to be like the standard long-distance runs we had done in the past, but it was only until the half-way checkpoint did the drama begin to unfold.

Before I continue, I must first explain that in the rules of the Comrades Marathon, there is a strict cut-off time at the half-way checkpoint. No runners are allowed to continue once the gun is fired there. Secondly, many athletes fail to reach this point, due to straining muscles or cramps, leaving them to run or walk it off. All without aid from their Seconds, or spectators, lest they be disqualified.

Here, I witnessed (on several occasions) runners picking each other up and carrying those injured over the line. Earlier I used the word 'drama', but this is not the best word to describe it. 'Camaraderie' or 'comradeship' would be more accurate. I suppose this is why the run is named the Comrades Marathon. Adding to these moments were the big crowds along the route, cheering and encouraging the runners—

despite their exhaustion—especially near the finish line.

This urgency and determination, to keep putting one foot in front of the other, turned my thoughts to the first Marathon run in 490 BC. To when the Athenian messenger, Pheidippides, ran forty-two kilometres between the bay of Marathon and Athens, to deliver the message of victory—even though he never recovered from an injury of his previous run, a few days prior, between Athens and Sparta. Only a few hours after delivering the message did the Athenian army rush back to their undefended city as the Persians sailed towards it.

What thoughts entered those soldiers' minds as they ran? Were they of fear? Of arriving too late, finding their city in ashes with their loved ones dead or captured? To run that distance, especially after fighting a battle earlier that day, and still manage to reach the city in time. What a relief they must have felt! Each like winners of a race, maybe.

Today, most participants of Marathons feel a sense of victory, like those brave warriors of the past. While there are only a few who officially win the medals, others have their own goals. For some, simply finishing the race is an accomplishment.

Years later, I asked another friend, who participated in the recent Comrades Marathon, how he did.

"I did well," he replied.

"How well?"

"Three minutes."

"Three minutes to what?" I asked.

"Three minutes left before the cut-off time," he explained. To him, he was a winner.

I learned a valuable lesson then. No matter how high or low your goals are, always strive to achieve them with absolute determination.

The purpose of this book is my hope to inspire many long distance runners who read it, to cheer them on to keep pushing forward—even if someone else is ahead. The tables can be turned, like those Athenians so long ago. Men who were not professional soldiers, but ordinary citizens, that managed against all odds to defeat a much larger army, from one of the greatest empires of the ancient world. All that AND they still ran over forty-two kilometres afterwards, to defend their city, arriving with enough time to spare.

What a feeling that must have been!

# MAPS

SCYTHIA

CASPIA

CASPIAN SEA

ARMENIA

TIGRIS RIVER

ROYAL ROAD

AREBELA

MESOPOTAMIA

MEDIA

EUPHRATES RIVER

ZAGROS MOUNTAINS

SYRIA

BABYLON

SUSA

ARABIA

BABYLONIA

SUSIANA

PERSIAN GULF

MAP OF THE
PERSIAN EMPIRE
& LANDS TO THE WEST

to Thessaly

ERETRIA

THEBES

AVLONA

PLATAEA

Mt. Parnitha

MARATHON

Mt. Pentelicus

Mt. Aegalos

ATHENS

Piraeus

Mt. Hymettus

to Corinth
& Sparta

SALAMIS

PHALERON

AEGINA

SOUNION

To Miltiades
Cemetery of
the Soldiers of Athens

MAP OF
ATTICA
& SURROUNDING AREAS

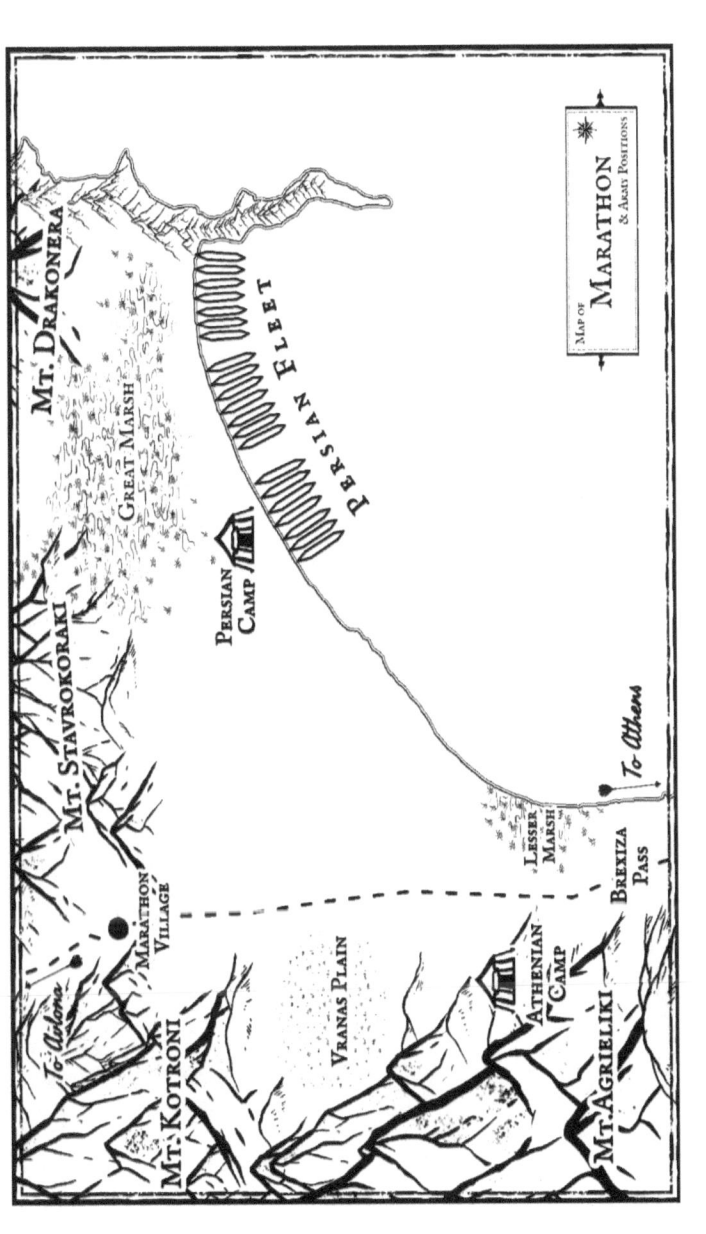

MAP OF

MARATHON

& Army Positions

MT. DRAKONERA

PERSIAN FLEET

GREAT MARSH

PERSIAN CAMP

MT. STAVROKORAKI

To Athens

LESSER MARSH

BREXIZA PASS

MARATHON VILLAGE

To Aphona

VRANAS PLAIN

ATHENIAN CAMP

MT. KOTRONI

MT. AGRIELIKI

# CHAPTER 1

The early morning sun scorched the palace of Susa with a fiery wrath. Artaphernes stood by an open window enjoying the gentle breeze coming from the Zagros Mountains, combating the sweltering heat of the desert.

Below, servants bustled about in the courtyard with their duties, trying to avoid the direct sun. They reminded Artaphernes of those he left behind in Sardis, people working hard to rebuild their homes after the Revolt.

*I should be there with them, helping them, leading them*, he thought, wiping beads of sweat dotting across his face with a cloth. Instead, he was stuck here. Waiting. For what, he was not sure. But one does not refuse a royal summons by the king.

He dusted the pristine white military uniform that clung to him. Not for the fiftieth time, he loosened the collar. A rash was forming. The last time he wore this uniform was at his father's funeral. Then, it felt normal. Now it felt like he wore someone else's skin, strangling him. Yet, despite his discomfort, his stature remained unbroken. Disciplined.

A knock came from outside his chamber's door.

"Yes?" He asked, going to the door.

"My Lord!" A staunch voice answered. "We are here to escort you to the Grand Hall."

"Very well," Artaphernes said, opening the door. Four guards in their bronze scaled armour stood awaiting him. Each equipped with a spear and shield. "Lead the way."

They marched through the labyrinthine halls in silence, save for the clatter of the guards' armour, passing many splendid works of art. Paintings, wall murals, frescoes, and statues depicting of kings long past and triumphant battles. However, none were more splendid than the palace's architecture. Great bulls sculptured into the carved stone pillars, their horns holding the support of the roof. Artaphernes thought of having the builders back home do the same.

Soon they arrived in the First Court where massive doors leading to the Grand Hall stood before them. Majestic lion sentinels carved into its dark wood, eagle wings spreading from the lion's backs, reaching to the ceiling. In front of the immaculate doors, men stood guard with a herald, wearing finely woven yellow robes, reading from his scroll.

The officer from Artaphernes' escort hurried towards the herald and after a few hushed whispers, the herald signalled to his servants, who opened the doors while he ushered Artaphernes in.

"General Artaphernes, Satrap of Lydia," the herald announced.

Voices of a hundred conversations welcomed him as he entered. Guests sat among three tables organized into a 'U' shape, like a horseshoe, each with plates, cups and utensils of the purest silver. A magnificent throne stood at the centre of the high table in the back of the Grand Hall, with widows behind bathed it in divine light. Soaring eagles were carved into the throne's backrest, with two lions flanking the seat— acting as arm rests—their maws open.

"General Artaphernes," a servant bowed. "Please. If you would?"

Artaphernes nodded and followed him along the right-wing guest table, greeting dignitaries— renowned generals and commanders—as he passed. Across from him, on the left-wing table, sat high-ranking officials. Both sides were filled with people whose names were known across the empire.

*What is going on? This is more than a mere summons. And for what purpose am I here?*

To the right of the throne, sat Mardonius, Chief-General and the king's son-in-law. He spoke to Artabanus, Head-Advisor to the crown and the king's brother. He sat to the left of the throne.

At each end of the high table, sat the two crown princes, Artabazan to the left of Artabanus, and Xerxes to the right of Mardonius. Both stared daggers at each other in silence, while attempting to maintain composure as they listened to their uncle's and brother-in-law's conversation.

When Artaphernes neared the end of the guest table, he paused for a moment. The servant was directing him to a seat of honour reserved only for those of importance among the guests. Next to his seat, sat Fleet Admiral Datis while across the hall, in the mirror seat along the left-wing table, sat Hippias—the notorious exiled Tyrant of Athens.

Artaphernes nodded a greeting to the admiral as he sat. An unnatural humidity, despite the arid climate, clawed into the airless room. Sweat beaded across his brow once more. It took all of his strength to appear calm and composed. Disciplined.

Trumpets and buccinae blared as the great wooden doors flung open. All guests stood, straight as the support pillars, when the herald declared, "Glory to his Magnificence! Darius the Great, King of Persia!"

Darius entered. His dominating presence calling all to submit to his authority. Robbed in an illustrious crimson velvet with an elegantly groomed beard, boasting such finery—an envy to lesser kings.

All bowed their heads in reverence as he passed. A battalion of guards and servants trailed behind him, stationing themselves along the hall's edges. To Artaphernes, it appeared as though the heavens illuminated the king' path to the throne, with a divine glow emanating as he sat. Two servants rushed to his sides, carrying ostrich feather fans, waving them and blowing the heat away.

"You may be seated," the herald instructed.

They all sat when more servants arrived with jugs of fresh juices, while others laid baskets of fruits and cheeses across the tables. Aromas of fresh bread and pastries filled the air, blending with other smells of roasted poultry—chicken, duck and quail.

*All the empire's mightiest men, together in the same room…all for breakfast?*

Slowly, conversations began once more as the guests recovered their composure while they waited for the king to pick the first portions. Artaphernes took a sip from his cup, letting the sweat liquid soothe his dry throat, when an elderly servant approached the king's side. It was too far for Artaphernes to hear. Darius stood, the high table shaking and all fell silent.

"Say it. Louder," the king commanded, gripping his goblet. "For all to hear."

The elderly servant bowed. "GREAT KING, DO NOT FORGET THE ATHENIANS!"

His words echoed throughout the palace and a grin broadened across Darius' face.

"Eight years! Eight years since the Ionians rebelled. Ravaging our western lands with the Athenians and Eretrians. Their time has come! Since quelling the rebellion, I tasked my servant to remind me every day of my fury. GENTLEMEN! I command each of you to consider the Ionian Revolt an insult your pride and the pride of our empire!" Darius paused. "However. Before we discuss such matters, let us enjoy this *lavish* feast. We shall continue afterwards."

Taking his seat again, the king helped himself to the contents of his plate. The guests attended to their own plates in silence, but soon a thousand conversations filled the hall—all discussing the king's words while servants laid food across the tables. Artaphernes studied those around him, contemplating as he sipped from his goblet.

*Is this why he's called us all here? To go to war with Athens and Eretria? But then why bother with me? Clearly there are others better suited for this endeavour.*

Once he might have been eager to do so, but since inheriting his father's duties, he never partook in military activities.

"At least there are some of us taking his majesty's words into careful consideration," Datis commented.

The admiral next to Artaphernes looked worn, tired, dark circles plaguing his eyes, as if he never slept for many nights.

"Excuse me?" Artaphernes asked.

"Of all the generals and commanders here, you alone are in deep, silent thought, while the others are ready to draw swords, hungry for glory. Even Hippias smiles at the prospect of war against his own people."

Artaphernes glanced at the exiled Tyrant, talking with a young official from Syria. His smile revealing a ragged tooth, giving him the appearance of a rat too excited for food.

"Not surprising," said Artaphernes. "He has been eager to regain his lost position. Would you also not be smiling like so if you were him?"

"If I were him, I would not have lost it to begin with. Even if I did, it would be because of my death."

"I heard you nearly did…" Artaphernes regretted his words as he spoke them, letting his discomfort get the better of him.

Datis grunted. "Yes. Mount Athos. The disaster that costed our fleet." He spoke as if he'd said these words a number of times. "That storm came from nowhere, claiming too many vessels and far too many good men. We spent nearly two years to rebuild what was lost."

Artaphernes stared in shame at the untouched food on his plate.

"Apologies," he whispered. "I, of all people, should know the challenge of rebuilding."

The admiral signed. "Do not trouble yourself over it. It is an expected topic of discussion when I am near. Even the youths at the end of our table are whispering about it."

Artaphernes looked to the two young commanders whispering in each others ears. They both looked away when their gaze met Artaphernes'.

"Although," the admiral continued, "my own disaster recovery pales in comparison to the one in your hands."

Artaphernes smiled softly. "There is not much difference in truth. I have the benefit of using old foundations to work with, sometimes entire buildings. Sometimes, none."

"Such is the aftermath of war," Datis said, raising his goblet to Artaphernes.

"To those of us who must rebuild," he replied, returning the gesture. They drank deeply. The cold liquid quelling his thirst. "Changing the topic, do you think his majesty will join in this campaign?"

The admiral pondered for a moment. "Not until an heir is announced. No. I imagine he will send Mardonius in his place once more. The Chief-General has been itching to return now his injury is healed."

"Wait, I thought his majesty already chose Artabazan. Last I heard, many pledged for him since he is the eldest." Artaphernes looked to the princes of Persia staring at each other.

"I am afraid that is stale news. Prince Xerxes has gained more popularity due to him being the firstborn after his Majesty's coronation. Artabazan was born before."

"I see. His mother, the Lady Atossa, is also Cyrus the Great's daughter. I guess from that alone, many would see Xerxes as the rightful heir."

"Precicely. Also many may not admit it, but it is clear to see Xerxes is also favoured by his Majesty."

"Hmm..." Artaphernes thought. Datis was right. Even now, the king showed his preferences as he conversed more with Xerxes. *Probably he still requires those who support Artabazan hence why he has not chosen yet.*

In silence, he returned to his food hoping to calm his nerves from the talk of politics. He spread creamy butter over the warm, soft, freshly baked bread, the flavors melting on his tongue. The fruits were juicy and sweet while the tender roasts flooded his senses with flavour.

He ate while talking with Datis about other minor topics, feeling himself calm until he noticed Darius looking at him with a smirk on his face. Had he been watching this whole time?

Before Artaphernes could process, the king turned to answer a question from Artabanus, his advisor. All the fine food turned bitter in his mouth and the cold drink clogged his throat.

Once all had their fill, servants came with bowls of warm water for the guests to wash their hands. Darius watched patiently while the tables were cleaned until only jugs and goblets remained. The king nodded to the elderly servant from before, who left briefly to return with others carrying scrolls and other documents.

They all perked up as servants placed maps of the empire's western half onto the tables. From the Zagros Mountains in the east, to Ionia, the Aegean Sea and the Hellenic lands beyond in the west. Small dots with names marked major cities across the empire with dashed lines indicating the main roads. Artaphernes felt homesick as he gazed to the dot representing Sardis.

The servants withdrew and Darius stood.

"Gentlemen! As stated before, the time has come for Eretria and Athens. Once we set them as an example, the other city states will not oppose us!"

He paused briefly to gaze at each of them, yet lingered when looking to Artaphernes.

"For this, I have spent the last eight years preparing. Our campaign into Thrace was a success, giving us access to the northern lands—despite Mardonius' injury and the disaster at Mount Athos."

Datis shifted silently in his seat while Mardonius only nodded.

"However," the King continued, "some changes have been made. First, although Chief-General Mardonius has recovered, I feel the need to rest him further. Thus, in his place as commanding general, I propose Artaphernes to do so."

Cold hands clung to Artaphernes lungs, forcing him to stand. Immediately coming back to his senses, he bowed.

Darius nodded and allowed him to sit once more before moving on.

"As many know, his father and my beloved brother served me well. Aiding me after King Cambyses passed away, helping my rise to the throne against Bardiya, the Usurper. For his service, I entrusted my brother to the Satrapy of Lydia until those rebels brought it near to ruin."

Images of a flaming city flooded Artaphernes' memories. Of him leading a charge against ordinary folk who got caught in the rebellion. People he had known. His stomach felt sick. He continued to listen to the King to distract himself.

"Once the rebellion was quelled, I tasked him with the restoration of Lydia. A task his son took with absolute fervour. I am confident in his leadership, and his sense of duty speaks for itself. He, of all here, have more reason to strike back at those who aided the rebellion." The King paused to catch his breath. "If any wish to object, now is the time."

The hall was silent as a crypt as Darius gazed at them seeking anyone who would oppose him. None dared.

"Good," said Darius, nodding. "The second decision I have made is that Admiral Datis is to ferry the army across the Aegean, as none know the sea better."

Datis stood, bowing elegantly. Darius nodded and the admiral sat.

"Finally," he continued, "Hippias is to accompany them as his advice, knowledge and influence would be invaluable with many followers in both cities."

A loud burst came from the left-wing table where Hippias quickly stumbled to his feet, bowing.

*Looks like I'm not the only unexpected participant in this campaign.*

Darius nodded, with a slight look of disgust and disappointment seeping through the immaculate figure.

"In return, I have agreed to appoint him as Satrap of Greece where there is talk of possible silver mines, and their marble is of exceptional quality. That concludes the introduction…now let us plan for there is still much to discuss."

All nodded in agreement. Mardonius was the first to raise his hand.

"Your majesty," he began. "If this campaign is to be a success, we cannot afford another disaster like Mount Athos, and we will need a safer route into Greece."

Many looked to Datis, but it was Hippias who raised an arm in response. Darius nodded and the exiled tyrant cleared his throat.

"Your highness, I agree with the Chief-General. The surrounding seas of Hellespont are known for such bad weather, and ferrying men across is far too risky, as proven by the last campaign. Might I suggest a different approach?"

"What do you have in mind, Hippias?" the king asked.

"Simply that we embark from Samos instead, and sail through the Icarian Sea to Naxos and Delos before heading to Eretria while subjugating islands along the way," suggested Hippias.

Darius considered for a moment before asking, "What are your thoughts, Chief-General Mardonius?"

"The proposed route would be safer and plenty of islands offer shelter from storms. It also allows another hold onto the west by sea. Besides, I am sure Admiral Datis is familiar with those waters…"

"Admiral?" the king turned to Datis.

"I know them," he replied with a heavy breath. "I do have a concern, however. The purpose of ferrying across the Hellespont is to field a large army and still supply it. Sailing directly across the sea will limit our forces and supplies."

Darius thought for a moment. "In your last report of the fleet's progress, you mentioned a capacity of at least forty thousand."

"Forgive me, your majesty," the admiral said, "but that report was based on an estimate of ferrying men alone. If we include supplies along with horses, that number drops. Especially with horses, since the animals take large amounts of room and are difficult to handle when carried across large distances by ship. In order for us to field a large force with the necessary supplies, we will have to limit their number."

"Which will be an issue," Artaphernes whispered to himself. Shock gripped him when he realized he spoke too loudly, and all were staring at him. He cleared his throat.

"I apologize for interrupting, I meant no disrespect, your majesty, but what Datis raises is a bigger issue. The core strength of our military lies with our cavalry and by extension our horses. Without them we will suffer heavy losses."

Darius nodded his head and thought for a moment. "Admiral, if we were to limit our number of horses to a few hundred, how many men can you ferry with enough supplies?"

"We have six hundred vessels ready to sail. Of those, we need two hundred for supplies. We can reserve fifty for horses, leaving us with three hundred and fifty vessels which roughly has a capacity for thirty thousand men. However, I am still reluctant to do so as what General Artaphernes said is correct. Without enough horses, the campaign will surely fail."

"Very well. Are there any suggestions?" Darius asked.

Mardonius raised his hand. "Your majesty, we could always raid villages for them. Though the likelihood of success to do so is slim as many will flee with their livestock upon hearing of our coming."

"If I may again?" interrupted Hippias. "Most villages in Greece are decentralized and isolated enough that it takes weeks for news to travel around. If we are quick enough, we may be able to accomplish these raids."

An older commander next to Hippias raised his arm. "If we do so, what happens if the enemy attacks us during one of these raids?"

"I doubt they will be foolish enough," Mardonius assured. "Even if we don't have cavalry, our sheer numbers alone will give them pause. The smarter move would be to defend their cities from the walls and wait for reinforcements."

"Speaking of," said Darius. "Hippias, how many allies do Athens and Eretria have? Which states will come to their aid and how many will they send?"

The exiled tyrant cleared his throat. "O-Our primary concern will be the Spartans since they have close relations with Athens. The others…not as much. Aegina and Athens are in lock-heads, Corinth will be hesitant and secure their own borders, while Plataea will send a token force of a thousand as per their treaty. However, Sparta…Sparta has five thousand ready to march, so my sources say."

"And how many defend Athens?" asked Mardonius.

"According to tradition, each of the ten tribes is to recruit at least a thousand men each in times of war."

"So, ten thousand," said Artabanus, the royal advisor. "Sixteen thousand in total, with aiding forces from Sparta and Plataea?"

A smile dashed across the king's face. "Sixteen thousand! We still outnumber them almost two-to-one! But tell me Hippias, are your sources still certain about Eretria?"

"Yes, your highness. My followers in Eretria have already begun their task of persuading the city to our cause once we arrive at their gates."

"Good! This is good!" Darius laughed. "Hippias, you have done well! Are there any other suggestions you have for us?"

"Of course…If I may?"

"Speak!"

"Yes, your highness. Most of the mainland is rocky with rough and uneven terrain, especially the shores where most of it is unsuited for disembarking an army. Athens, even more so, since its harbour has been reinforced against naval attacks–or so my colleagues claim."

"So, then what is your proposal?"

"North of Athens lies a bay near the village of Marathon. It is well sheltered from storms with a decent coastline for ships. A number of large hills surround the area with a road leading into the western passes, past many isolated villages, towards Athens. It is the perfect place for us to disembark."

"Hmmm…" Darius mused, stroking his beard. "General Artaphernes! As commanding general of the campaign, what are your thoughts?"

Artaphernes studied the maps, staring at Greece and the bay mentioned by Hippias.

"It appears ideal for disembarking; it is close to Eretria and allows the army to march on Athens while Admiral Datis blockades the city from sea."

"Which puts immense pressure onto the Athenians," Datis agreed. "Hopefully enough for Hippias to convince them to surrender."

Artaphernes nodded. It was a good plan, all things considered. Yet, anxiety and worry still gnawed on him. Many things could go wrong, costing his head if they did so.

"GOOD!" Darius thundered, the high table shaking as he stood, turning to Artaphernes and Datis. The light from the window behind blocked, casting a dark shadow over them.

"Gentlemen!" he said and the three stood. I will leave it to you!"

His voice then changed to a low, menacing growl. "I want every single hostage from Athens and Eretria to be brought before me on their knees begging for mercy! THAT is my command! *Do not* disappoint me!"

"Yes, Great King!" they said in unison, bowing.

An icy shiver crept into Artaphernes' bones with spidery tendrils. Nausea clogged his throat as memories of war and carnage flashed before his eyes. He almost gagged thinking how much innocent blood would be shed.

Nothing prepared him for Darius' plans to lead an army and conquer two cities deemed enemies. Yet despite how sick he felt, he would obey and fulfil his duty.

As the discussions continued, only one thought–one question–still burned in Artaphernes' mind.

*How long will this war last?*

# CHAPTER 2

A warm summer wind blew through the fields of golden wheat, the stalks dancing gently in the breeze. Simon stretched his crooked back, feeling the years creep on him like the balding patch on his head. He gazed over the fields while others around him continued to cut. They had made staggering progress. It would be a prosperous harvest.

Pride and gratitude filled his aching bones. Always, he reminded himself of how fortunate he was to own such a field.

Arable land was scarce in Athens and wheat only came as an import from other city states or from Egypt, which were costly. However, his locally grown crop could be sold much cheaper and meet the demand.

*But first we must complete what we started,* he thought. *For that we need extra hands… Where is that son of mine!?*

Down the hill, into the valley he looked, where the city could be seen with the sea behind it and the island of Salamis on the horizon. A cart drawn by two mules crested over the nearby hill coming towards them.

Simon whistled, calling the men nearby while waving his straw hat.

"The cart is here! Time for lunch! Call the others!" He yelled.

They gathered by the roadside and waited, some carrying their tools while others collected theirs together and left them. Soon the cart came close enough to see the ladies sitting in the back with baskets on their laps. They seemed to be listening intently to a young, dark-haired woman in her early twenties sitting next to the driver.

She gestured dramatically as she spoke, pointing to her cheeks and right eye before they all broke into a gale of laughter. When she turned around, Simon only saw the little girl she once was, smiling at him.

Daphne had always made him proud, helping wherever she could, even helping on the farm from time to time without complaints.

*Only if Damon was the same...*

Before the cart stopped, Daphne leaped out and darted to Simon flinging her arms, with the basket, around him.

"I've brought lunch," she said, stepping back and handing him the basket and a fresh water-skin.

"I see that. Thanks," he said, smiling.

Inside he found fresh bread neatly packed with pieces of boiled chicken, a few olives and some cheese. They walked together to his favourite spot under the shade of a nearby tree overlooking the valley.

"Tell me, where is your brother?" he asked, breaking a piece of bread and giving it to her.

"Damon's at home still in bed," she replied casually. "He came home last night in a terrible state."

"Hung over again?"

"Worse."

Simon sighed. "What did he do this time?"

"Apparently, he got into a fight and by the looks of it, he came second best. I think if you saw him, you would either laugh or cry."

Simon sighed again. "And Lydus didn't help him? They always go drinking together."

"Well, you see, that's who he fought."

"*What*!?" Simon yelled, nearly choking on an olive. "How? Why? They grew up together, practically they are brothers! What possessed them to fight?"

"Well, I can't be too sure yet, but I have a suspicion it's over a woman. The other ladies agree, stating 'men only do such stupidity over a woman'. Even if this is so, I'm not sure who they are fighting over either."

Simon sighed a long sigh, rubbing his now aching head.

"Well… Thank you for telling me. I'll have a talk with him once I get back home," he said. "Let your mother know lunch was delicious as always."

"Will do!" she said with a smile. "I'll be sure to prepare your bath too. Also, mother is preparing lamb for tonight."

"My favourite. I'll be looking forward to it."

She hugged him once more and darted off to the other woman, talking with them until it was time to head back.

Simon sat under the shade of his tree eating the rest of his lunch and watched them descend into the valley of hills below until they disappeared. After some time gathering his thoughts, he put on his straw hat before walking to the fields with the others. He picked up his sickle and went back to cutting the beautiful golden stalks.

Whatever went through his son's head, he prayed he could muster the strength to deal with it.

They worked until the sun slowly descended into the western horizon, filling the skies with hues of red, orange and purple. A southern breeze brought the smell of salt and sea.

Simon did a final check on the fields while the men loaded tools and bushels of wheat onto the cart. It would still take a few days to complete the harvest.

He washed his hands and face with the last drops of water in his water-skin and climbed into the cart heading home with the others. Thankfully, it would be a short ride home since he lived close by.

"Good work today, everyone," he said. "If all goes well, we should be done within the next eight days. But for now, let us all get home and enjoy some rest. We've earned it."

They nodded their heads and smiled, making merry small talk along the way. Soon, Simon climbed off and watched the cart go into the night.

Outside his home stood a woman with dark, black curls wearing a light blue dress waiting for him. Her smooth skin glowed in the warm light spilling behind her. Helena was as beautiful as the day they married.

"Welcome home dear," she said, her voice like honey. "How were the fields today?"

"Good! It was good. We've made much progress. Though I hope we're able to finish soon," he replied, climbing the short steps to the front door.

They embraced, her scent of lavender and lemon almost drowning him. Unfortunately, it did not last long.

"Daphne has drawn your bath and laid out some fresh clothes for you," she said.

"Reliable as ever. She'll make someone happy someday," he commented.

"Ha! Whoever marries her will have to mind his tongue or he'll be very sorry."

They both smiled and walked through the door in each other's arms. Down the corridor they went, before she parted to the kitchen where Daphne helped prepare the meal while he went for his bath.

Fatigue and the aches his muscles endured melted away in the hot water as his body sunk in. A hot bath after a hard day of work was the best.

Steam rose from the water's surface, filling his lungs and clearing his now relaxed mind. If he was to clean up his son's mess, he would need a clear head.

*Best not wound his pride further, he must feel humiliated enough as is. I need to be delicate. But I also need to know what happened!*

*...First, I'll get the story from him and see what I can do from there. I should also see Ariston tomorrow and see if we can't calm the waters.*

Through the window he stared at the moon rising into the night sky as he soaked. If there was any man who would listen to reason it would be Ariston.

Like Damon and Lydus, he and Ariston grew up together—even fought side-by-side. Their families had been tied ever since. Simon could not allow such a disaster to cause a rift between them.

Soon, the water cooled too much before Simon decided to get out and dry himself, dressing in the clean clothes left neatly folded by Daphne. He finished when he heard Helena announce, "Dinner is ready!"

At the dining room, he found his wife and daughter waiting patiently with a table full of food and drink in front of them. He sat next to Helena and stared across the table to the empty chair.

"Where is Damon?" he asked.

"Still in his room," replied Helena, filling his cup. "He's been in there all day."

"I'll get him," Daphne said, and before anyone could say a thing, she left only to quickly return with a smile. "He's on his way."

Not long after, Simon saw a dimly lit figure linger in the doorway outside the room's light.

"Come on dear, before the food gets cold," Helena said, dishing portions of lamb.

Damon limped into the room, dark bruises covering his face with a cut lip and an eye so swollen it almost looked like a blue tangerine. He sagged into his seat, turning to his side, trying to avoid everyone's stares and hide in the shadows.

Simon then recalled his daughter's words, 'You will either laugh or cry.' He did both.

"Who made you look like this?" Simon asked, wiping away his tears.

No answer.

"Damon…" he said more seriously.

"Lydus..." Damon whispered.

"Lydus?" Simon asked, curiously. "Yet I thought he was like a brother to you. I never could imagine the two of you wounding each other this badly…Why? What happened?"

Silence.

Simon thought Damon would remain silent, when a flood of answers came.

"I don't know! We went drinking last night and Lydus kept insulting me for some reason. Mocking me! I tried to ignore him at first, but he just kept going, until…until…AH! I don't remember anything other than that!"

Simon saw the fury and frustration, the guilt and shame, in his son's eyes. Even if he never told the full truth, until it emerged. Simon needed to believe in his son and give him the benefit of the doubt—as a father, he had to.

"Alright then," Simon sighed. "Tomorrow, you will stay home and rest. But the day after, I want you to go to Ariston and apologize. Even if you didn't start the fight, it's time to be a man and end it. Afterwards, I expect to see you in the fields to help with the harvest. Are we clear?"

"Yes… Father," Damon replied, looking down.

"Good," Simon said. "Now then, let's eat."

***

Early the next morning, Daphne left on a cart heading to Athens and the Piraeus markets. The fishermen returned at this time with their latest catch, and if she needed to be there first if she wanted the best.

People bustled about, crowds flowing through a river of streets when she arrived at the markets with stall owners crying out their wares. It would be easy to get lost in this maze, but Daphne knew them well—and her keen sense of smell directed her to the fish market.

"Sardines! Get fresh and delicious sardines! Fresh catch this morning!" roared a burly man, behind his stall stacked with various fish—mostly sardines.

Putting on her best smile, she skipped forward. "Morning Demetrius, hope your catch went well."

"Ah, morning Daph! Was wondering when you'd show up," he said, smiling broadly. "But, yes, our catch went extremely well! Just look at all the sardines we netted not so long ago!"

"Hmm," Daphne thought for a moment, putting a finger on her pouting lips. "How much for a dozen?"

"Only five drachmas."

"Five!?" she gasped. "And no discount for a beautiful lady and a regular?

"Oh, don't go giving me those big sad eyes. My daughters use them all the time."

"Because it works," she said, pouting her lips further.

"Ah, alright! Twist my arm, why don't you!" He sighed, leaning over his stall, "tell you what. Just for you I'll lower it to four—but only because you're a regular customer. If I go any lower, I'd be robbing myself, and my poor daughters won't get a thing—even if they gave me that look."

"It's still worth a try," she said, getting her money and handing it to the fisherman.

"I thank you kindly," said Demetrius, putting several sardines in a sack and giving it to her. "Here you go. Do tell the folks I said hello, and I'll drop by to get some more wheat."

"Of course," Daphne said, putting the sack in her basket.

"And also tell your lazy brother to grow some sea legs and join me on the next run!"

She giggled. "I'll try, but you might have to wait some time before he gets on any boat."

"Oh?" he asked with a raised eyebrow.

"Maybe a tale for next time. Thank you, Demetrius."

"Anytime!"

She waved the fisherman goodbye before losing him in the crowd, only hearing his yells of sardines. While walking back to the cart, a familiar voice caught her attention.

Around a bend she found Cassandra desperately haggling with another fisherman. By the sounds of it, he priced his sardines much higher than Demetrius.

Her haggling came to an end when Cassandra noticed Daphne and caved into the fisherman's price, grabbing the sack of sardines and stormed over to Daphne.

Daphne just smiled. "Morning Cass-"

"We need to talk!"

"Sure. I wanted to speak with you too, but can we walk and talk?" Daphne asked. Cassandra nodded and the two left the fisherman.

"Those two bull-heads need to grow up!" Cassandra burst. "Lydus came home two nights ago with a face covered in so many bruises you'd think his natural skin colour was blue!"

Daphne chuckled. *It seems Damon gave as good as he got.*

"What's so funny!? Do you have any idea how much of a pain it was to keep the cut above his right eye clean!"

"I'm sorry," said Daphne, still recovering herself. "It's just…Damon also came home in a similar state."

"Ugh! I swear those two become more childish as they get older! It's barely been a year since their 'horse race'! As if the damage to my father's vineyard wasn't enough!"

"Now it's a competition of fists," commented Daphne. "Though I am still wondering what the prize is this time."

Cassandra sighed bitterly. "Lydus told me last night when I changed his bandages. Apparently, they're both '*in-love*' with Hermione, Philip's daughter…The idiots! She knows she's pretty and plays all the boys and our brothers are falling for it!"

"I suspected it was over a woman, but unsure who…"

"Does it matter who!? We need to stop those two before any more damage is done! If only…"

A young man flew around a corner, crashing into them.

"Apologies ladies, I have urgent news to deliver!" he yelled while dashing off into the city.

"Watch where you're going!" Cassandra yelled. "Idiot. I swear some – oh no. I know that smile."

"I have a plan," said Daphne with a smirk. "I'll visit you later to discuss it. We'll need to keep the details between ourselves. In the meantime, we need to keep the two apart. Agreed?"

"Agreed," Cassandra said, raising an eyebrow. "Whatever you have planned, I almost feel sorry for the bullheads... almost."

"Alright then, I better get back before these go off," Daphne said, lifting her basket with the sardines.

"Yes, I'll see you later today then," Cassandra said, nodding.

The two ladies parted to their separate carts going back home. With the plan she thought of, Daphne was sure it would put an end to their brothers' pointless disputes.

*It must.*

*** 

Late afternoon came when Simon spotted a horse with a familiar rider. He left the shade of his tree to greet the traveller, taking his water-skin—brought by Daphne earlier, who left in a hurry with a grin that worried him.

Once the rider got close enough, Simon saw the stern face of his friend, now plagued with new wrinkles and newer grey hairs. Yet, he still rode with such stature, making young men look frail.

"Good day, Ariston!" Simon greeted, once his friend arrived. "Always good to see you."

"Good day, Simon," his old friend greeted back, climbing off his horse. "I have come to discuss some family matters."

"Of course," replied Simon, gesturing with his hand as a welcome. Ariston nodded and the two walked, touring the fields.

"I see you have made much progress," Ariston commented.

"Hopefully, we'll be done before the autumn rains. Though I wish Damon could be around to help…"

"Speaking of," Ariston coughed. "I came to discuss our sons'…altercation… We have been comrades for many years, and it would be a shame to see it end over a squabble between boys."

"Agreed. Daphne seems to think it's over a woman, but I haven't confirmed anything yet."

"Whatever the reason. We *must* calm the waters. Should the two find themselves on the battlefield, they will need to have each other's backs, not their throats."

"And it's not like we're getting any younger either," said Simon, stretching his back.

"Speak for yourself."

"At least my hair hasn't gone grey yet."

"What hair?" Ariston asked and they both chuckled as they arrived at Simon's spot under the tree.

Before Simon could retort, a column of dust rose from the road, rumbles echoing through the valley below. Simon squinted to see several riders galloping across the country.

"I wonder what their rush is?" Simon asked.

"Messengers from Athens," said Ariston. "Quick, one comes this way."

They hurried back to the roadside where Ariston's horse nibbled on nearby hay, arriving at the same time as the messenger.

"Greetings, good sir! What brings you all the way here?" Simon asked.

"Good day, gentlemen. I bring dire news from Athens!"

"Why? What has happened?" asked Ariston.

"A vessel from Samos arrived earlier this morning, its crew warning us that a large Persian fleet has set sail towards us. A meeting is to take place tomorrow morning at the Agora. Now, if you would please excuse me gentlemen, there are many others I must inform. Good day."

The messenger pulled his reins and galloped back to join the others heading west.

"This is bad," said Ariston. "Persia has not forgotten Ionia. They will be coming for us and Eretria."

Simon stood in shock and in horror. He could barely grasp his breath let alone speak. All around him, the workers watched. He could see in their eyes, the same fear he felt.

He sighed, mustering his courage and stood as straight as his back would allow.

"You all heard! Persia is coming! Tomorrow, I will attend the meeting and relay all that is discussed. Until then, we must finish as much of our work as we can!"

"Come on," yelled an elderly farmhand. "We best get back to it before either the rains or those savages get here!"

The others nodded in stunned silence before returning to the fields, working even harder than before. Simon turned to Ariston, who already mounted his horse.

"I must ride back to the vineyard and warn the men there as well. Farewell, Simon. I shall see you tomorrow at the Agora."

"Farewell, Ariston," Simon replied. "And may Hermes bless you with his speed."

Ariston nodded and galloped away, back to the main road heading north. Simon slowly wandered to his tree, gulping down the remnants of water in his skin and grabbing his sickle.

*It doesn't just rain, does it?* He thought, returning to work with the others.

*Athena protect us!*

# CHAPTER 3

Crowds flocked through the streets of Athens towards the Agora, murmuring. The air felt still, like the moment before a storm.

*Or just before a war*, Simon thought as he walked alongside the crowds of the city's main road, the Panathenaic Way—somewhat glad to finally stretch his aching legs from the ride down. *This is precisely why I prefer traveling by cart.*

Up the road ahead stood Ariston, talking with two other members of their tribe, Cleanthes and Glaukos. He could hear bits of their conversation as he got closer.

"…Are we even in a position to fight?" Cleanthes asked nervously, shifting his weight from one thin foot to the other.

"What choice is there? The Persians are coming whether we are prepared or not," replied Ariston.

"I heard some suggest we surrender on good terms, like in Ionia," Glaukos commented, who towered over the other two.

"Absurd! If we surrender, the Persians could do what they wish to us! Even if," he paused. "Ah! Simon has arrived. Good morning."

"Morning, morning," Simon greeted, joining the group.

"Morning, Simon," the other two greeted in unison, and they all joined in the crowds towards the meeting.

"I hope I didn't keep you waiting too long," Simon said, scratching his head.

"We feared you may have gotten lost," Ariston teased.

"I almost did. Athens has grown since I was last here."

"So, Simon," Cleanthes asked, "what are your thoughts on the upcoming war with the Persians? Because our dear Glaukos here reckons we should surrender."

"No, I didn't!" Glaukos protested. "I only said that some suggested we should surrender and try to bargain a good deal with the Persians to leave us in peace."

"That's ridiculous!" Simon laughed. "We'd be selling ourselves into slavery!"

"I said much the same," added Ariston. "Besides, I am certain those who proposed such a notion were the aristocratic snakes still in Hippias' pocket."

"*That* should make Themistocles happy," Cleanthes muttered. "He's been arguing with them for so long."

"I doubt anyone is happy with this situation," said Simon. "Our clan leader especially."

"At least we were able to fortify the harbour against attacks," said Glaukos.

"But if the Alcaemonidae would just stop fighting with him just because he's a commoner then maybe we wouldn't be in this mess," Cleanthes grumbled.

"I think we would still be in this mess regardless," said Simon.

"Perhaps, but we would at least be better prepared for it," added Ariston. "But that is just politics for you."

"Yes, poly-ticks," said Cleanthes.

They continued to walk and talk until they arrived at an open clearing under the shadow of the Acropolis, filled with people from all corners of the city and its countryside.

At the centre of the clearing, a large platform had been raised with ten seats and a podium. Like a temporary amphitheatre, benches were organized around the platform into ten sections—one for each tribe.

The four walked to the section dedicated to the Leontis tribe and joined their kinsmen. While weaving through the rows, Cleanthes pointed behind the platform.

"Look! You see that!"

"What?" Simon asked, squinting to see. "It's just Themistocles talking with someone."

"Yes, but do you see *who* he's talking to!?"

"Is that Aristides?" asked Glaukos.

"And they're not fighting?" Simon added.

"That is a first," said Ariston. "Goes to show how great of a threat Persia is."

"Do you think they've come to a truce then?" asked Cleanthes.

"We'll have to wait and see," said Simon. "But if we are to survive, we'll need them both."

"Only one way to find out," Ariston added, finding suitable seats near the front.

Not long after, Themistocles and Aristides broke their conversation and joined the other clan leaders who began taking their places on the platform. Once the final stragglers arrived, the Agora buzzed with conversation when a giant of a man walked onto the platform and stood behind the podium.

Callimachus, the Polemarch, War Archon of Athens, gazed over his audience.

"CITIZENS OF ATHENS!" His voice thundered, and all fell silent. "Today, we gather to discuss the future of our city and her people! I'm sure all are aware of the approaching threat sailing towards us! Upon hearing the news, I sent the messenger, Pheidippides, to Sparta to call for their aid! In the meantime, we must choose one to lead us against the invaders!"

Callimachus turned to the ten men sitting behind him, "Gentlemen, I would call on one of you to do so! Do we have any nominees!?"

Themistocles stood. "Athenians! In the past, I warned this day would come! The day Persia would seek their vengeance against us! Many ignored me then. Do not do so today! After much time in thought pondering over this, I can think of no other best suited to lead us against Persia than the man who once fought for them! I nominate Miltiades of the Philaid Tribe!"

Gasps and murmurs rushed through the crowd. A member of the aristocratic Alcaemonidae tribe in the audience stood.

"Outrageous! Miltiades is a traitor! A sell out!" He yelled. "Let us not forget that he once ruled the colony of Chersoneses as a tyrant under Hippias! Feigning sorrow for his brother's death before imprisoning his own men! All that *before* he knelt to the Persians!"

"Only because they took his lands and forced him to become their vassal!" protested a member of the Philaid tribe.

"Yes!" Another joined. "Not once did he take up arms against Athens! How could he be a traitor!?"

"Didn't he also rebel against the Persians in Ionia!?" yelled another.

"Meaning he's prone to betrayal!" yelled the Alcaemonidae member. "Who is to say he won't betray *us*!"

The crowd devolved into bitter bickering with thousands of differing opinions clashing against one another.

"Well, this is getting us nowhere," Ariston whispered.

"CITIZENS!" Roared the War Archon, his voice trailing as an echo into the city. Simon was sure even the Persians could hear it.

"The case of Miltiades and his loyalty concluded long ago, and he has been found a defender of Hellenic Freedom! Let us not bring old conflicts to cloud our judgments! If you disagree, then nominate another and let the people decide!"

"Very well," said the first Alcmaeonid who started the argument. "I nominate Xanthippus to lead us!"

The crowd buzzed once more in disbelief with only a few others from the Alcaemonidae nodding in agreement.

"What's going on?" asked Glaukos. "Isn't Aristides the Alcmaeonid's general? Why would they nominate Xanthippus?"

Ariston shook his head. "It appears that Aristides 'The Just' isn't as popular anymore."

"But why now?" Simon asked. "Why cause such turmoil now, at a time when we need to be united?"

"Perhaps, it's those still under Hippias who are trying to cause as much chaos as possible," suggested Glaukos.

"Only fools' debate over a house while it burns," said Ariston.

"Bloody politics," grumbled Cleanthes.

"Whatever is going on, Themistocles looks like he has a plan," said Simon and the four watched the platform eagerly.

The Leontis tribe leader seemed to smile, like a hunter watching their prey fall into a trap.

"Xanthippus is still too young and inexperienced!" Themistocles replied to the Alcmaeonid. "He may one day grow into a fine general someday, but right now, does he know the Persian army!? Its tactics!? Its weaknesses!?"

The Alcmaeonid stumbled over his words for a retort, but Themistocles continued.

"Right now, we need Miltiades! He is the best choice!"

Before the crowd could break into their own conversations again, Aristides stood, waving for silence.

"Citizens!" he spoke in a loud, confident, yet calm voice. "Now is not the time to play politics! The Persians are at our doorsteps while we argue over trivialities! Need I remind you of who our enemy is!? We are against, not another city state, but an entire empire! One that has dominated the majority of the known world! Xanthippus certainly has potential, but I still find myself in agreement with Themistocles! We cannot afford mistakes! So, I ask you all to consider carefully before casting your vote!"

Aristides went back to his seat and, what seemed to Simon, nodded to Themistocles who nodded back. Whatever they planned before the meeting, it seemed to work.

Callimachus looked at them and turned back to the crowd. "Very well then! Are there any other nominees!?" he asked. When none answered, he continued. "Then shall we vote!? Those in favour of Miltiades!?"

Thousands of arms raised to the sky across the Agora. All except the few Alcaemonidae voted in favour.

"There we have it! I see no need to vote any further! Miltiades has been chosen to lead!" Bellowed Callimachus, turning to the ten men behind him. "Now then, gentlemen, there is still much to discuss, and time is short! Shall we begin!? Yes, Stesilaos!?"

One of the ten raised their hand. "Before we start, there are many here who think surrender would be the wiser option to prevent unnecessary bloodshed…"

"You cannot be serious?" Miltiades asked, who had been silent until now. Sighing, he stood, turning to the generals. "Who among you agree with Stesilaos' proposal of surrender!?"

Five of the ten men raised their hands, though some looked reluctant to do so.

"Then it appears we are in a predicament," said Miltiades in annoyance. He turned to Callimachus. "As War Archon, it is your duty to decide in such circumstances. To choose to either surrender and restore Hippias to power under an even greater despot or to fight! To cower away and be known as the man who let freedom die or be its champion! Do we give into tyranny once more or do we leave a legacy as those that fought against it!? Do we let Athens crumble away or let her grow to become the pre-eminence of Greece!? The choice is yours, Callimachus. All hangs on you!"

Simon could only hear the sound of his breath and heartbeat. Callimachus stared at Miltiades and approached, towering over the aged general.

"I am the War Archon of Athens! Her greatest warrior! The *Polemarch*!... How could I possibly retreat before a battle!? WE FIGHT!"

Everyone in the clearing erupted into cheers and shouts of excitement. If anything, Callimachus knew how to inspire the fighting spirit within men.

Miltiades, smiling, turned back to the other five who disagreed. "There we have it. We have chosen to fight. So, shall we now work together and plan our victory?"

They nodded in stunned silence.

"Good! Then to begin with, each of us needs to recruit at least a thousand men from our respective tribes."

"We also need as many allies from the other city states," Themistocles added. "Since Callimachus sent Pheidippides to Sparta, we should hear from them within the next day or two."

"What of the other city states?" asked Stesilaos. "If we're going to fight the Persians then we will need to send messengers to them too."

"I doubt Corinth will answer and will likely wait out the storm instead," replied Aristides. "And due to the animosity between us and Aegina, I doubt they will even consider our pleas."

"And Thebes is too far. Their troops won't make it in time," added Miltiades.

"What of Eretria?" asked Cynaegirus, general of the Eupatridae tribe. "From our current reports, the Persians will be attacking them first."

"Then we should send some men to aid them," said Aristides.

"If we're able to defeat the Persians there, then there won't be any need for us to worry about a battle here," said Themistocles.

"But if they fail, it will leave us weaker with less men," Stesilaos added.

"Even so, it could still give us more time to prepare as well," Cynaegirus replied.

"Very well," said Miltiades. "Those in favour of sending men to aid Eretria?"

Eight hands rose.

"If the Persians are planning on attacking Eretria first, they should arrive within the next five or six days," said Miltiades. "Callimachus, can I ask you to find as many ready and willing men to travel to Eritrea as soon as possible?"

The Polemarch saluted with a smile. "They're as good as already being on the road!"

"Good! I want them to be there waiting by the time the Persians arrive. In the meantime, I want the rest of us to begin arranging supplies and recruits. We shall meet once more once Pheidippides has returned from Sparta."

They all nodded in agreement, even those with doubtful expressions. Miltiades turned to the crowd.

"ATHENIANS!" He announced in a voice loud enough to almost compete with Callimachus. "As you have chosen me to lead and fight for this city, I can only do with as much as you can give! Those willing to fight, I urge you to volunteer with your tribe leader! Those already prepared for battle are to see Callimachus after, to travel to Eretria and aid our brothers there!"

He cleared his throat and continued. "The rest should spend their remaining time with friends and family, get their affairs in order and prepare equipment! As commanding general, I give you all my word: we will defeat the Persians and protect our home! We shall meet again in three days once

Pheidippides has returned! Until then, may Athena grant us victory!"

With the final words echoing through the Agora, people began making their way to their homes to deliver the news of what happened—the fire of hope rekindled within many. Yet worry and doubt still clouded Simon's mind.

*I guess we'll just have to have a little faith*, he thought. *Not much else we can do.*

# CHAPTER 4

Damon awoke to the rooster's crow, his head pounding from the screeches. Why couldn't that bird stay asleep until after the sun rose!?

He shifted out of bed carefully, trying not to aggravate his wounds any further. Thankfully they weren't as tender as the day before—when he was stuck in bed.

*Bloody Lydus! You'd swear his fists were made of marble!* He thought. *Was there any need to hit that hard!?*

Dishes rattled in the kitchen, most likely his mother and sister preparing breakfast.

*Not only the bird, but the women as well!* He thought, dressing himself slowly, wincing every time he exerted a muscle too much.

Once dressed, he hobbled over to the dining room to find his father, waiting patiently at the table with four bowls and wooden spoons already set. The old man seemed to lose hair by the day with a wrinkle to replace it.

*Seriously!? Does no one but me sleep in this house!?*

"Good morning, Damon. Strange to see you up so early. How are your wounds today?" his father asked.

"Morning," he replied, rolling his neck, trying to hide the bursts of pain spiking up his head. "Much better."

"Good. We'll need all your strength today. There's much work to be done before…"

"Ah! Damon! You're up early!" said Daphne, popping into the dining room with a pot filled with porridge.

"Well…I decided it best to get up early if I'm going with father to the fields," Damon said, sitting in his place.

"What? Finally decided to become a productive member of society instead of lazing around, drinking all day?" she asked teasingly.

"I don't always do that!" he protested.

"Weird. I could have sworn it was you I kept finding in a drunken stupor at a tavern every night for the last two moons."

"Not every night!"

"Being stuck in bed all day recovering from a dumb fight doesn't count."

Damon sighed. "I've said, a million times by now, that it wasn't my fault."

"Still doesn't stop father from losing hair over it. I mean look at that poor scalp…"

"Daphne," their father warned sternly. "Enough."

"What!?" she asked, gasping, putting on her most innocent face. "I'm only teasing him a little."

"But do we really need to start the day with it?" their mother asked as she entered with a jug of juice.

"I guess not…"

"Good morning, mother," Damon greeted her as she and Daphne sat.

"Good morning, dear. How are your wounds?" she asked.

"Better."

"Good. Now with us all here, I suggest we eat before it all gets cold."

They began to eat while talking about the latest news and gossip. Most were either uninteresting or about the harvest's progress. Only once were the incoming Persians discussed, but the topic quickly changed to more gossip.

Damon mostly kept to himself, eating in silence, only giving his opinion every now and again.

With an empty bowl and a full stomach, he felt more human than a wounded animal—ready to face the gruelling day ahead. He and his father continued to prepare for the day while his mother and sister cleaned up and began cooking meals for lunch and dinner.

Soon the cart arrived, already carrying farmhands along with some of their wives and a few of their daughters too. Damon and his father climbed into the cramped cart.

If it were any other time, he wouldn't mind since he sat next to a pretty girl who couldn't stop giggling looking at him, but instead he sat in silence.

"What's on your mind?" his father asked.

"Nothing much," Damon replied with a shrug.

His father looked at him. "You've hardly spoken this morning and you've been tapping your leg since breakfast."

Damon sighed. "Well…it's just that…you've been in battles before and…"

"So that's what's going on. Yes, I've seen my fair share of war, though most of those were against other city states. Persia is a much greater foe."

"How so?" Damon asked, a fragment of annoyance building. "Aren't their soldiers no more than slaves fighting for loot while we fight for freedom?"

His father sighed. "Half true. Some do fight for the spoils of war, but most of their soldiers come from conquered nations. Taken from young ages and trained in the art of war, not knowing anything else. But wars aren't won by soldiers alone."

Damon sat back in silence. "Alright. Any advice then?"

"Only to keep a clear head and trust your comrades. Don't be reckless and keep calm. I've seen too many die from carelessness or cowardice."

*Me? Coward!?* Damon thought in annoyance.

"Those who've never seen battle tend to soil themselves when the time comes," his father continued. "Though, if you follow what I've said, you'll survive it."

Damon wanted to scoff at the notion but thought better of it. Just as well he did, they arrived at the fields still needing to be reaped. No matter how annoyed he was, he wasn't in the mood to argue with the old man.

Instead, he clenched his jaw and jumped out of the cart with the others, grabbed a sickle, listened to a speech from his father, and started cutting.

*Survive!?* He thought, hacking away. *I'm not some snivelling child who hides behind his mother's skirts!*

The bruises across his face should have proved that much at least. He was a man now. Deserving of respect.

"Well, if it's proof they want," he grumbled to himself, "it's proof they'll get. Just wait. I'll claim the head of a commander and then we'll see who's still a child."

Sometime later, when the boiling sun reached its zenith, his father whistled, signalling to take a break. The cart arrived with the ladies bringing lunch.

Damon found a shady spot under a tree overlooking the hills, wiping away sweat from his sunburned skin and stretched his back. It ached even worse than any cut or bruise he received from Lydus.

*No wonder the old man stoops. Hopefully I won't experience* that*! Well, I shouldn't have to become a renowned warrior,* he thought when his sister came and handed him a basket and a water-skin.

"Thanks," he said, gulping down the cool water, washing his face and hands. Never would he imagine water tasting better than any liquor until now. His stomach growled at the smells coming from the basket.

While eating, his sister leaned and whispered in his ear. "I have some news that might interest you."

"What news?" He asked with a full mouth.

"Daphne!" A woman by the cart called waving.

"Looks like it's already time to go," she said, standing.

"Wait! What news!?"

"I'll tell you later," she said, darting off to the old man and hugged him before jumping into the cart.

*What was that about?* He thought, watching the cart descend into the hills below.

He sat in silence, enjoying the fresh bread and fruit when his father joined him.

"I see you've found my favourite spot," he said, sitting next to Damon. "If we continue at this rate, we should finish within the next three days."

"Just in time to join the army…" commented Damon.

"Yes…speaking of. Tomorrow, I want you to stay home and prepare our gear. The swords and spearheads will need resharpening and a good polish. Armour also needs a few dents to be hammered out."

"I thought you desperately needed my help with the fields?" Damon asked.

"I do, but it won't do us any good if the Persians beat us because we failed to maintain our equipment."

"Alright then," Damon sighed.

*At least I won't have to spend the day being tormented by heat and grass.*

"Anyway, we best finish up and get back to it before the Persians get here," the old man said, getting up.

*Hooray, back to torture*, Damon thought dryly, also getting up and leaving his lunch basket with his father's following him back to the field with the others.

Late afternoon couldn't come sooner, but when it did, Damon sighed with relief. Finally, his day stuck in the furnace was over! All he could think of was a hot bath and his bed. However, he would still have to wait.

He joined the others to pack away the sickles and other tools used and load the last bushels onto the cart to be carried to storage. Once done, he climbed on, and the journey home began. His father congratulated the workers for their efforts, and they should enjoy the upcoming rest.

Once home, Damon immediately went for his bath, bliss filling him as his worries melted away.

*At least I won't be out there again tomorrow,* he thought. Thankfully maintenance of their equipment was much easier and more comforting for Damon. *Maybe if I finish early, I can visit Phillip's for a quick drink.*

Eventually, the water got cold enough to notice, and he decided to get out, drying himself and dressing in the toga left neatly folded by his sister.

*Now that I think about it, has she been avoiding me since I got home?* Was this piece of news that important? *Or is it another one of her pranks…*

With his toga wrapped tightly, he left for the dining hall and sat, waiting until dinner was ready.

After eating, he finally caught Daphne alone in the kitchen washing dishes.

"So…What's this super important news you were supposed to tell me about?" he asked.

"Shh!!! she jumped, spinning around. "Not so loud." She bolted to the door, looking up and down the hallway.

Damon raised an eyebrow. "What's with all the secrecy?"

"I just don't want anyone else to hear."

"Really? Hear what?"

"You know Xenophon? Your old school mate?"

"What about him?"

"He proposed to Hermione…and she said yes. They're planning to marry after the war."

Damon stood still, mouth agape, his mind too stunned to even process what he heard.

"So?" he finally managed, trying to sound casual. "Good for them…But what does this have to do with me?"

"So, you could watch over him during the upcoming battles. He's part of the Leontis tribe, so you'll be fighting side-by-side," said Daphne. "Who knows what terrible grief will befall poor Hermione. Imagine the tragedy of losing your beloved before your own wedding?"

"Oh alright, fine! I'll watch over him!"

"You better. Also, don't tell anyone else. I promised I wouldn't do so."

"Promised who?"

"Can't say. I do promise the information is credible from someone close to Hermione's family. Now promise me!"

"Fine! I promise! It's not like I'm some loose-lipped gossiper who tells her brother private information."

She punched him on the shoulder.

"Ow," Damon said, rubbing his arm.

"Don't. Tell. Anyone! I know where all your bruises are."

"Alright! Not a soul."

"Good," she said, smiling at him with complete innocence when their mother walked into the kitchen.

Daphne continued with the dishes as if nothing happened. Damon left for his room as quickly as he could, laying in his bed and staring at the ceiling. His mind pondered what his sister told him.

Grief hit him, like a maelstrom of daggers tearing at his chest. Sore muscles or broken bones could be compared to it.

Memories of Hermione drifted into his mind, her smile, her laughter. The day they first met, all the time they spent together. He remembered how they childishly promised to one day wed. Now, she was promised to another…

Damon silently cried himself to sleep that night.

He awoke the next morning to find himself alone at home. His mother and sister likely already left for the markets while his father toiled in the fields. Cold porridge waited for him in the dining room.

When he finished eating, he decided it best to do his chores—anything to keep his mind busy—and went to the spare room they used for storage. It didn't take much rummaging to find his father's war gear and his own, gifted to him some years back on his eighteenth name day.

The bronze armour glistened in the sunlight. No scratch or dent tainted it, unlike his father's, which showed its age—much like the man himself.

Next to the armour, he found a pair of swords and spears behind two round bronze shields.

A rooster's crow snapped Damon's thoughts back and he got to work. Polishing and cleaning, knocking the few dents he could from his father's armour. The swords and spear heads were dull from negligence and would need to be taken to the smiths for resharpening.

Damon sighed.

*Might as well get going*, he thought, grabbing the blades and spear heads before leaving the house.

Since they lived closer to the fields meant they lived further from most others. Thankfully, the nearest smithy wasn't too far away. Damon enjoyed the pleasant walk down, glad the pains and bruises in his feet were gone.

Soon, he arrived at the smithy to find a long line ahead of him, forcing him to sit on a bench and wait patiently.

He sat in solemn silence, watching the apprentices run up and down while their masters worked. The rhythmic *cling* of the hammer on metal drowned out his thoughts.

"Morning Damon. I see you also brought your things for repair," said a familiar voice coming from the head of the line.

"Lydus!? Didn't expect to see you here."

"And why not!?" Lydus asked, sitting next to Damon. "I've got to fight too, remember. Not like I have a choice in the matter."

"At least it gives us a chance to make a name for ourselves."

"I'm just happy to stay alive, honestly. And…well…truth be told, I'm terrified. I just don't know if I'm capable. I mean, what if something happened to me, or my father? Who would look after the family?"

Damon rubbed his jaw. "Well, judging from the last time we saw each other, I'd say you'll be fine. In fact, I'd hate to be the Persian on the other side with you coming at me."

Lydus smiled, showing a gap where a tooth once was. "Well...you're not too bad yourself. A bit too aggressive, in my opinion, but still a good fighter. I'll be glad to have you by my side."

Damon smiled. "Same. And who knows? With the two of us fighting side-by-side, we may even bag a commander's head."

Lydus chuckled nervously, scratching his chin. "Tell you what Damon. Let's leave the battle when we get to it. Nothing will be the same after. So, until then, let's keep these final days peaceful?"

"Alright! But you better be ready when the time comes."

"Definitely...by the way...did you hear about Hermione?"

"What about her?" Damon asked, feigning ignorance.

"Apparently, she's getting married to our old school mate, Xenophon. They're planning the wedding for after the war."

A sharp pain struck Damon again hearing those words. "Well...good luck to both of them, I suppose."

"But I thought..."

"Thought what?"

"Never mind. Anyway, it looks like it'll be your turn next," Lydus said, pointing to where the line was supposed to be.

Damon turned back to find it gone. He quickly grabbed his gear and stood by the doorway to the smithy and waited while an apprentice serviced the man in front. Before long, it was Damon's turn, and he handed his gear to the apprentice.

"Listen," said Lydus, waiting by the door, "it was good talking to you, but my equipment has already been seen to, and I have to head back."

"No problem. I guess I'll see you some time then."

Lydus nodded. "Hey, how about we go out later tonight for a drink?"

Damon hesitated for a moment. "Would love to…but I told my old man I'd help around the farm…besides, I doubt any innkeeper would let us in after the last time."

Lydus chuckled. "We'll have to be on our best behaviour next time…then I guess I'll see you at the camps?"

"Of course! And when the battle begins, those Persians won't know what hit them!"

Lydus smiled. "Well until then," he said, extending an arm to Damon.

"See you at the camps," Damon replied, and the two friends shook hands.

He watched Lydus go until the apprentice returned with the newly sharpened swords and spear heads. With everything going on, Damon felt glad he and Lydus restored their friendship—especially now there was nothing to fight about.

The gaping hole still ate at his chest every time he remembered Hermione's face.

*Maybe once I become a renowned warrior, then Hermione would reconsider. Maybe if I can prove myself a hero.*

*Maybe…*

# CHAPTER 5

Crowds gathered at the Agora once more for the follow-up meeting. Three days had passed since the last one and the people were eager to hear Sparta's response. Simon and Ariston quickly found their seats near the front again and waited.

On the wooden platform, the ten generals sat while Callimachus walked behind the podium as everyone settled.

"CITIZENS OF ATHENS!" The War Archon began. "We gather again as a continuation of our last meeting! To start, Pheidippides returned last night with great news! Sparta will answer the call!"

Cheers and sighs of relief blew through the crowd. However, it was short lived.

"Unfortunately," the Polemarch continued, "they will only be able to come once their religious festivities are over, after the next full moon! Until then, we must defend our city!"

All sank into uncertainty again with one question on everyone's mind, could they fight long enough to buy time?

"Reports also reached us that the Persians are only a day away from Eretria! We've sent a small, elite force to aid in their resistance! With any luck, they'll hold, giving us time to prepare!"

Some sparks of hope returned, but much dimmer than before.

Callimachus turned to the ten men behind him. "Gentlemen! In our last meeting, we each agreed to recruit at least a thousand men! I assume you have all completed this!?"

They nodded.

"Good! Then let us begin today's agenda! Miltiades!?"

Miltiades stood. "Gentlemen! Our first point of discussion is the location of battle!"

"That should be obvious," said Stesilaos. "We stay behind our walls and defend the city from within."

"Yet that would endanger our citizens and trap them with no place to evacuate," Miltiades replied.

"So? What then? Open battle?" Cynaegirus asked.

"That's insane!" yelled Stesilaos. "We would be exposed to their cavalry! Not to mention they outnumber us!"

"But what if they don't have cavalry?" asked Themistocles.

All looked to the Leontis general.

"Gentlemen, we forget the route the Persians took for this campaign," he continued. "They sailed across the Aegean, unlike before where they would ferry their men across Hellespont and march down. Instead, they sailed across the sea!"

"Themistocles is right," Aristedes added. "If they sailed directly here, then they would be limited in supplies and capacity! Meaning, they either are fielding a smaller force…"

"Or they didn't bring enough horses for an effective cavalry to go with a larger force," finished Cynaegirus.

Miltiades smiled. "Exactly! The Persians won't have enough space for a large army and horses for cavalry!"

"Which would leave them needing to scour the land and raid villages for the beasts," Themistocles said.

"And they cannot waste resources in unnecessary skirmishes either," added Aristides. "They undoubtedly know of the harbour's reinforcements as well."

"If they do, then they wouldn't want to waste their time and numbers trying to land there either," said Cynaegirus.

"Right!" said Miltiades. "Therefore, I believe the Persians won't attack Athens immediately by sea, but rather disembark elsewhere and march on the city while raiding along the way."

"Then we need to figure out where they will land," Callimachus commented.

"The only place they can. Gentlemen, I believe they will disembark at the bay of Marathon!" said Miltiades.

Themistocles nodded, considering for a moment. "It is near Eretria and not too far from Athens either, also providing decent cover against storms. Not to mention, the waters are deep and wide enough for their ships too."

"There are also many villages along the way," Aristides added. "It does seem like the perfect place to land an army."

"So, what if we get there first and block all roads leading to Athens?" Miltiades asked. "Hopefully, that will buy us enough time for the Spartans to arrive."

The generals nodded in consideration. All, but Stesilaos.

"It is a sound plan. *If* they did land at Marathon," he said. "What if they don't? We would be leaving Athens defenceless!"

"If they did decide to attack the city instead, we could just run back," said Aristides.

"And if they split their forces?" asked Stesilaos. "One to attack Athens while the other lands at Marathon?"

"Then we have two weaker armies to defeat. We just deal with one before the other," replied Themistocles.

"They wouldn't do that anyway," said Miltiades. "The Persians prefer to march under a unified front. If they did split their forces, the main bulk would still attack by land with a skeleton crew managing a blockade by sea."

"Besides," Aristides added, "it would be a logistical nightmare to maintain both armies."

"Alright," said Stesilaos. "But what if they decide to attack Athens after seeing us all at Marathon?"

"Good question," said Miltiades. "This brings me to my next reasoning. If they do decide to attack the city instead, then we send a messenger back to warn our citizens and give them a chance to evacuate."

"Giving us an opportunity to focus on the Persian army without needing to worry about our citizens' safety," said Aristides.

"If anyone here has a better plan to guarantee our citizen's safety *and* provide good chances to stall the Persians for time, we are all ears," Miltiades said.

None spoke.

"Personally," said Callimachus, "I like this plan of yours!"

"Then we are in agreement?" Miltiades asked. They all nodded. "Alright then, it is decided. Are there any other concerns?"

Themistocles raised a hand. "As we know, there are two routes between Athens and Marathon. Since we are pressured for time, I suggest we march through the shorter road past Cephisia and the hills north of Mount Pentelikos."

"But that road is too treacherous," said Aristides. "We won't be able to take our wagons through there, never mind run."

"Which adds to my point," said Themistocles. "While we take the shorter route, the wagons take the eastern passes between Mount Hymettus and Mount Pentelikos. We should also ensure the path is clear for a run back as well."

"Which also adds to what I wanted to bring up," said Cynaegirus. "Since we aren't too sure where the Persians will land, I suggest we make camp at Avlona. It isn't too far between Marathon and Athens and could give us a head start wherever they land."

"That is a good idea," said Miltiades. "We'll also be able to easily keep track of the Persian fleet since the nearby shores overlook the seas by Eretria. Now, if there's nothing else?"

They looked at each other and nodded their heads.

"Then we march in three days," said Miltiades. "In the meantime, I want scouts stationed to watch for any signs of the Persian fleet. Once they arrive, it should take them about two days to complete disembarking and another three for their men to be ready for battle. I'll begin setting up preparations at the north-east encampment site. With that I think this meeting can be concluded."

Callimachus smiled, turning back to the audience. "It has been decided! We march in three days! Until then, the army is to gather at the north-east encampment site! From there, we march to Avlona! I hereby call an end to today's meeting!"

The Agora began to disperse into the streets of the city below. Many still with heavy hearts, but now a small flame flickered with hope.

***

Simon and Ariston walked to the stables together and said their farewells to Glaukos and Cleanthes. After watching them go, the two friends left for the stables where they had left their mounts.

"I believe our sons resolved their differences," Ariston said.

"So, I hear," Simon replied. "Damon told me last night he spoke with Lydus while at the smiths. But I still wonder what truly happened between them."

"Does it matter? If they no longer hold any malice toward one another then we can move on."

"Fair enough. I just hope we can sort things out before the Persians arrive."

"I am sure we will," said Ariston as they came near a tavern. The sign outside swung with an image of Hermes above writing that read 'The Messenger's Rest'. "Say, would you care to join me for a cup of wine?"

Simon considered for a moment. "Why not? A drink might ease my worries."

Inside, they found it brimmed with customers who also came to drown their troubles. With some luck, they found a suitable table in an empty corner and placed their order.

Simon watched those around him drink in solemn silence, uncertainty in their faces. The same questions plaguing them, vexed Simon as well.

What does the future hold? Who will look after my family? Will they even survive? Is it possible to stop the coming threat? Can we win?

Simon's thoughts returned when their drinks arrived. The two friends toasted each other, sipping the deep, sour red.

"Tell me, Simon. What worries you the most?"

"With all that's going on? My son... He's still inexperienced, especially in war and I fear what will happen to him."

Ariston sat in silence for a moment. "Yes...I feel the same about Lydus. But I also worry about my wife and daughter..."

"Honestly," said Simon, "I'm far more concerned about Damon. Helena and Daphne know how to stay safe, but Damon...I just can't say the same for us heading into battle. What about you? Do you think we have a chance?"

"Well...I'm confident that we will drive the Persians back somehow. But if anything happens...In case anything happens, let's pledge to each other? If something happens to me, please look after Lydus and my family?"

"Alright," said Simon, stretching his hand out. "And if anything happens to me, please look after Damon and my family."

Ariston nodded, taking Simon's hand and they shook. "To our sons and family."

"To our sons and family!" they toasted, drinking deeply.

They continued to talk and drink for some time about the city, their families, reminiscing about old times and discussing the current progress of their respective farms.

When Simon emptied his third cup, he sighed. "Well, I guess it's time I get back. See how things are going."

'Yes. I suppose it's best we head out, before it gets dark. We should meet again like this once the war is over."

Simon nodded, standing. "Let's just pray we'll have a chance to do so...So long my friend, and thanks for the drink."

"Goodbye, Simon. It has been a pleasure. I shall see you again in three days at the encampment."

They shook hands again and embraced before parting their separate ways. Simon felt glad to speak with Ariston about his matters. A great weight lifted from his shoulders, yet he knew the worst was still to come.

He turned to look up the Acropolis, the small temple of Athena only barely visible.

*Despite all that is to happen, please look after Damon*, he prayed. *Please give him wisdom.*

# CHAPTER 6

Simon and Damon arrived at the north-east encampment during the early morning with a group of warriors. Six days had passed since the news of the invading Persian fleet first arrived.

Activity bustled throughout the encampment as men worked pitching tents, cooking breakfast, or doing exercises. A clash of swords, shields and spears could be heard from a nearby field where men trained and sparred—mostly new recruits.

"Ah! Simon!" called a man wearing an officer's uniform.

"Memnon! Good to see you!" Simon greeted, shaking the officer's hand. "How have you been?"

"As good as can be! Got a second daughter a few weeks back," Memnon replied, looking a mix of bashfulness and pride.

"Congratulations! To you and your wife."

"Thanks. Though…I do wish to see them again after the war."

"I'm sure you will…We all need to."

"...Anyway, you'll need directions to the Leontis section. It's that way," he pointed. "Ariston arrived last night and should have things set up there."

"Ah, thanks. Keep safe and may Athena bless you in the coming battles," Simon said.

"Same to you!" replied Memnon before Simon and Damon left the man in the directions he gave.

Soon, the Leontis campsite came into view, and they entered, finding Ariston and Lydus talking with a group of youngsters.

"Good morning, gentlemen," Arison greeted. He wore a similar uniform as Memnon. "I was just about to send this lot over to the training yard before breakfast."

"Good morning," Simon greeted back. "It's not a bad idea to get them into shape. Damon, why don't you join them?"

"Are you sure? Don't you need help with our tents?" Damon asked.

"I'll be fine. Ariston can help."

"...Alright," Damon said, offloading their bags and joining the other novices with Lydus as the two old friends watched them run off.

"Now then, follow me. I kept a space for you and your son," said Ariston, walking to an empty lot.

Simon followed and the two began their work pitching up the tents. Deft hands moved skilfully with experience and in no time, they finished.

"Phew," Simon sighed, stretching his back before sitting down on a small wooden stool. "Been a while since I set one up."

"Brings memories back, doesn't it?" Ariston asked, handing Simon a water-skin.

"Yes…" Simon replied, gulping down his water. "Anything interesting happen before we arrived?"

"Well, a messenger from Eretria brought news that the auxiliary force we sent three days ago are on their way back with some refugees."

"What happened? Surely Eretria hasn't fallen yet?"

"No, but I believe they think we are fighting a losing battle and wish to avoid pointless death. Our generals have been stuck in the command centre since last night discussing."

Simon looked towards the large tent in the encampment's centre, wondering what the generals were discussing at this very moment. He also wondered what his wife and daughter would be doing now—the Eretrians too.

"Well then," said Ariston, standing. "Shall we go see how our sons are doing?"

"Sounds good," Simon said, standing as well and the two began their journey to the training grounds. Along the way, Simon turned to his friend. "By the way, who is the current training sergeant?"

"Oh!? I thought you already knew...you will never guess who."

Simon raised an eyebrow. "Alright, let me think… is it Themison?"

"No. He currently serves as quartermaster."

"Lysagoras?"

"Stables."

"Glaukos?"

"Sentry duty."

"Surely it's not Cleanthes!?"

"Olympus no! I like Cleanthes, but the poor man is stuck with the crew digging latrines."

"Poor man indeed… Anyway, who is it?"

"Alright," Ariston sighed. "Timon."

Simon stared blankly. "You're joking right?"

"Not this time."

"Oh," Simon said, cringing. "I feel sorry for the boys. If there were any man more difficult to please, it would be him. I once argued with him over a sword I had sharpened, enough so to shave a man's beard. He then claimed it couldn't even cut cloth!"

"Yet, I have yet to hear of him losing a man under him. He may be harsh and hard to please, but he is one of the best to learn from."

Simon sighed. "I guess…you're right. The boys will need all the help and guidance they can get."

Sounds of metal on metal and the grunts of men grew louder. They crested over a small hill where a large field came into view below them. Wooden fences lined the field's perimeter with many men busy exercising while others practiced their battle formations.

Youths from all ten tribes gathered in a corner, two of them being yelled at by an older man in front, loud enough for Simon and Ariston to hear.

"You call that fighting!? Those barbaric movements!? My grandmother had more grace!"

In the ten years since Simon last saw him, Timon hadn't changed much—besides the few silver hairs lining his head. Otherwise, he still stood tall and straight with an impeccably shaved jawline. Not for the fortieth time did Simon's back ache, wishing for another's spine.

He chastised a youth which seemed to glare daggers at him while his sparring partner appeared pensive and nervous.

"What!? Timon sneered. "You think you're better than an old woman!? Prove it!"

The youth lunged his wooden sword at him, yelling. Timon simply stepped aside, leaving a foot out which tripped the youth over as he ran past, his partner staring dumbfounded.

"Did I not command that we fight in pairs!" yelled Timon.

"B-b-but two on one is unfair, y-you don't have a partner!" Stuttered the second novice.

Timon scoffed. "The battlefield is never fair! One-on-one duels without interference only occur in legend. But it's just as unfair for me to even get a decent warm-up from you two!"

"D-don't blame me if you lose some teeth."

"You have to hit me first."

"Aaaaagh!" Screamed the other youth, who came charging after getting up. He was trying for a thrust this time.

Timon turned his body sideways and blocked it with his wooden sword before striking a blow to the youth's gut.

"Thrusts and sneak attacks are only useful if you catch your opponent off-guard! Yelling just gives yourself away!"

Behind Timon, the second novice swung a broad overhead strike, but he stepped to the side again and the blow hit the youth in front of him, before countering with a strike to the knees, causing the attacking youth to fall over his partner.

Simon and Ariston continued to watch as they descended the hill. To them, it looked like two bulls trying to catch a cat.

"Looks like they are about to reach their breaking point," Ariston commented.

"Can you blame them?" Simon asked. "Remember how proud and impatient we were at that age?"

"Don't remind me. If it were not for Stephanus berating us, we would still be in there."

"Now they have Timon to do that. It took all I had back then to not lose my cool."

After a few more similar exchanges, the two novices found themselves out of breath and Timon out of patience.

"Go! Clean yourselves up and be thankful that I only left you with light bruises!" Timon commanded and the two walked off. He then turned to the others watching. "Tell me, what is the key to winning a fight?"

The group stared at him and each other, but none spoke up.

"Is it brute strength? Precise strikes? No! It's about reading your opponent and countering them! It's all a mental game! One you cannot win without using your head. Else you lose it. And we don't need headless men to defend our city."

A snort from the group caught Timon's attention. "You!"

Simon's heart sank when Damon and Lydus stepped forward. Timon glared at them in disgust.

"You think this is all a joke!? That you're here to be entertained!? If so, then go back home and enjoy your theatres and plays! The battlefield is no place for boys! It's a place where they go to die! It's my job to make sure you return as men! Now, I ask again, do you think this is all a joke?"

"No sir!" Damon replied. "I was just impressed with your movements earlier sir!"

"Is that so?" Timon asked, intrigued. "Do all the ladies fall for such smooth talking?"

Damon smiled.

Timon grunted. "It's one thing to be a good talker. Another to be a good fighter. You'll have better luck as a politician."

"Then let me prove it sir!"

Timon considered for a moment. "Very well. Then you and your partner are up." He looked through the group while Damon and Lydus walked towards him. "And you two as well!"

From the group, a youngster the size of Glaukos stepped forth—another with Cleanthes' stature at his side. Simon recognised the bigger novice as Xenophon, but the other appeared to be from another tribe.

"Begin!" Timon instructed and Damon rushed at Xenophon, who blocked the strike which quickly became a thrust blocked by Xenophon's partner, forcing Damon to retreat as Lydus parried the counter.

Xenophon's partner swiftly turned his attention to Lydus, preventing him from aiding Damon, who continued his attacks against the ever-defending

Xenophon. They were evenly matched, but Simon knew, eventually one side would give in.

He sighed when it came sooner than expected when Damon slipped on lose ground and fell, Xenophon's partner taking his opportunity while Xenophon blocked off Lydus from aiding.

Damon found himself lying on the ground with a wooden blade at his throat.

"Enough!" Timon commanded, stopping Lydus in mid-swing. The other two offered Damon a hand, which he refused. Sweat dripped from their faces as they lined up to face their instructor, panting heavily.

"Good bout, especially for novices, but novices you are still, and it shows!" Timon said, before turning to Xenophon's partner. 'Except you. You moved much better than the others… What is your name?"

"Ameinias of Eupatridae, son of Euphorion, sir!" he replied, saluting.

Timon nodded. "Ah! So, you're General Cynaegirus' brother? Your father has taught you well."

"Thank you, sir!"

"However, stop moving around so much! It wastes energy! If not for your opponent's carelessness, you would have tired yourself and the result would be reversed."

"I will work on its sir!"

"Good," Timon said, moving to Xenophon. "And you. You spent far too long on defence. Not once did you commit to an attack. Why?"

"I didn't want to hurt them, sir," Xenophon replied.

"And you think the Persians will care about such sentiments?"

"No sir! I have no problem attacking a Persian. But I won't harm an ally."

Timon stared at him. "Then best you start, else neither you nor your allies will learn."

"Yes sir."

Timon looked at him then turned to Lydus and Damon. "You two! Both of you need more training, especially you," he said to Damon. "You have no regard for your surroundings and rush without thought! Aggressiveness may be good for a fist fight, but it will kill you in a battle! Observe, *then* act!"

"Yes sir," Damon said with a frustrated look.

Timon turned to Lydus. "You, on the other hand, think too much. You were indecisive and hesitant, which cost you and your partner! There is no time in a battle to overthink things!"

Lydus nodded. "Yes, sir."

"Now then, since we have limited time, I want each of you and your partners to find another pair and spar! Those who've just fought may take a bit of a break, once done you will join the others! Now, begin!"

The novices quickly dispersed into various groups of four, two against two. Simon and Ariston went to their sons resting nearby, watching the others.

"Good fight boys," Ariston complimented.

"But we still lost," Damon replied, panting.

"Even so, you'll learn from it," said Simon. "That's the purpose of training. To learn and lose here so you don't later on."

"Simon is right," said Ariston. "If you boys keep pushing yourselves to improve, then you'll be ready for the battles ahead."

"Hopefully those won't come too soon," said Simon, giving his son a water-skin.

"If it's going to be this tough, imagine fighting someone in armour," Lydus commented to Damon.

"Maybe one from another city state," Ariston said. "But the Persian's armour has more gaps we can take advantage of."

"True, but they still outnumber us," said Simon. "In most battles, it's numbers that count."

The novices continued their matches until the last one concluded. Timon then gathered them again.

"That is, it for introductions! From today onward, we will work on ensuring you all aren't a complete disgrace on the battlefield! But much still needs to be done! To start, you all lack endurance because of your undisciplined lifestyles! However, I have the perfect solution!" Timon said, somewhat menacingly.

"From this day onward, before we begin training, all novices will run a lap around the entire encampment! The last to return will skip his next meal...well, what are you all standing there for!? Unless you all don't want to eat?"

They all dashed off, each trying to outrun those behind. Simon and Ariston watched as they disappeared behind a cluster of tents.

"That should keep them busy," said Timon, smiling. "And I see you two gentlemen have nothing better to do than watch me play with the novices. Simon. Ariston."

"Greetings to you too Timon," Simon replied sourly.

"Timon. Just keeping an eye on our boys," said Ariston.

"That so? My guess is it's the two who lost against the big one and General Cynaegirus' brother."

"That's them," said Simon.

Timon appeared unamused. "Now I know why I felt nostalgic looking at them."

"Will they be ready for the upcoming battle?" Ariston asked.

"No one is prepared for their first battle. But if they listen, they'll survive." said Timon just when the first few novices began reappearing on the opposite end. "It appears the camp is still not big enough."

Soon, struggling clusters poured in, those returning sat on the ground breathing heavily until, eventually, the last two arrived—one with blood running down his knee as the other held him up.

"Apologies for being a bit late, sir," said Ameinias, pushing the injured novice to the group first. "But it appears that I am the last to arrive."

Timon stared at him with a raised eyebrow. "And do you expect me to spare you because you're a general's brother or because you took care of an injured comrade?"

"Not at all, sir! If I am to miss a meal, then so be it!"

"Hmph!" said Timon, sounding unimpressed. "Very well then. The trumpets will sound soon for breakfast. When they do, you are to remain. As for the rest of you, once you are done eating, you will return here. Until then, dismissed!"

The novices broke into smaller cliques among themselves—most in the four-men groups who sparred each other earlier. Some went to refill their water-skins while others rested on the floor. Damon and Lydus spent their time with Ameinias and Xenophon, looking after the injured novice.

"Let me have a look," said Ariston and began tending to the wound. From all their years in and out of battles, Simon's old friend had picked up the art of healing.

Damon and Lydus seemed intrigued by Ameinias, who spoke highly of his brothers, General Cynaegirus and Aeschylus the Poet, who also joined the army to hopefully write a ballad about the upcoming battles.

Trumpets sounded and they all began up the hill towards the feasting tents, but before they got there, a second set of trumpets sounded. Simon and Ariston looked at each other.

"Which one is that for?" asked Lydus. "We aren't under attack, are we?"

"Calm down," said Ameinias. "That was a call for all warriors to gather outside the command centre."

"Why? What for?" asked Damon.

"It seems our generals are done with their discussions." replied Ariston.

Simon sighed. "Hopefully with good news."

They journeyed through the camp, following some soldiers forced to leave their meals behind. Soon they arrived at a clearing in front of the huge tent of central command.

Callimachus stepped out with the ten generals behind him and waited until the crowd was large enough.

"ATHENIANS!" His voice thundered. "I apologize for disturbing your meals this morning, but this news cannot wait! Last night, reports came in from Eretria that the Persians have landed! They have sent our men back along with their refugees! They should arrive later this afternoon!"

Uncertainty took the crowd.

"Therefore!" The Polemarch continued. "We have decided to march to Avlona the day after tomorrow and give them a day to recover and for the others to gather! Until then, begin preparations! Dismissed!"

The crowds dispersed back into the camps below where the news spread. Later that afternoon, the auxiliary force Athens sent, arrived with some men from Eretria while the rest of the refugees continued towards the city.

Finally, when evening came, Simon sat next to his son by the fire. He seemed exhausted.

"Never expected training to be so tiring?" he asked.

"Never expected that much running," Damon replied. "My lungs feel like they're on fire!"

"You'll get used to it as you build stamina. It's always a good thing if you can hold on longer."

"I just wonder how long Eretria will hold on," said Lydus, staring into the flames.

"With luck, long enough for the Spartans to arrive," Ariston assured.

"And what if they don't? What if they're overrun or surrender before then? What if…?"

"They'll hold," Ariston repeated. "Focus on your training for now and leave the 'what-ifs' for the oracles."

"How can you be so sure?" asked Lydus.

"Because they are brave men," said Ariston. "They'll fight for as long as they can until their families are safe."

"Many of their women and children have already arrived in Athens this afternoon," said Simon. "Others have fled to Thessaly."

"And what will happen to those unable to flee?" asked Lydus.

"Should Eretria fall, they will either be killed or taken prisoner to be sold as slaves," answered Ariston.

"Then all the more reason we need to win," said Damon.

Simon smiled. "We must win. Else our families face those atrocities too."

"I'll die before I let that happen," said Ariston.

"Same here," said Simon. "We'll protect our home."

"And drive them back!" Damon said. "One thing is certain, win or lose, I'll fight to the bitter end!"

"Please don't let that end come too quickly," warned Simon, staring at the moon above.

*Almost full*, he thought. *Just a few more days and the Spartans will be here.* He looked back at Damon, trying to cheer Lydus up.

*Athena, let them be on time!*

# CHAPTER 7

A large, white marble building peaked through the rocky gaps of the mountains—a sanctuary dedicated to Heracles.

"Send word that we shall rest here and await the others," Miltiades ordered a messenger. Soon the long column of Athenian soldiers halted, gathering around the sanctuary.

Miltiades watched them as they flooded in. Never did he expect the road to Avlona to be so perilous.

Although their route was shorter, many loose and slippery rocks covering the landscape slowed them down. At their current pace, the wagons would arrive before they did. If not for the men constantly helping of each other, things would have been much more difficult with more injuries. All it took was one wrong step.

North-East, a column of dust rose from the horizon. Trumpets blew the familiar rhythm signalling allies.

*It appears we have some guests.*

"Miltiades!" Callimachus called, running to him. "It's the Plataeans! They've come!"

"Then shall we go meet them?" Miltiades asked and the Polemarch smiled broadly.

Morale soared from the men as they heard the news. Now, all they needed were the Spartans.

Not far ahead, the Plataeans waited with their commander at their head.

"Greetings!" The Polemarch welcomed.

"Well met," the Plataean commander returned with a salute. "I am Commander Arimnestos of Plataea! I have brought a thousand men to answer the call of Athens in these dark times!"

"Welcome, Commander! I am Miltiades of Philia, Commanding-General of the Athenian defence! We graciously accept your aid and hope to fight alongside you in the coming battles!"

"As do I", said Arimnestos, shaking Miltiades' hand.

"Come commander. Rest your troops while we discuss matters. You must all be exhausted from your journey."

The commander nodded and called his men forth, letting Miltiades and Callimachus lead them through the Athenian forces. They shared information with each other of the Persian movements and the ongoing siege in Eretria.

Once the sun peaked at midday, Miltiades gave the order to march on, only arriving at Avlona at sunset.

Miltiades stood in the command tent the evening of the day after, overlooking maps of the Marathon plains–courtesy of the Athenian archives.

"…Fires light the night sky from the coast, and the reports coming in from men sent across the channel…" the scout paused.

"Thank you," said Miltiades. "When ready, return to your post and keep watch on when they begin boarding once again."

"Yes sir!" The scout saluted and left.

Miltiades turned to the other generals with him. "We will need to move at once when we have confirmation. In the meantime, we must prepare for our arrival at Marathon."

Stesilaos shook his head. "I still think they will attack Athens instead."

"Especially if they notice us at Marathon," Cynaegirus agreed.

"Then I take it you have a solution, General?" Miltiades asked.

"I do," Stesilaos answered. "I suggest we fortify our position at the base of Mount Agrieliki along the southern road."

Themistocles nodded in consideration. "It is a good defensive position giving us visibility of the bay."

"It also blocks the long road south towards Athens," said Aristides.

"And even if the Persians decided to take the northern road, we would know," added Callimachus.

"I doubt they would use that road anyway since Hippias knows how treacherous it is to march an army through those mountains," said Themistocles. "We only managed because our men are familiar with the terrain.

"Speaking of," said Cynaegirus. "These marshlands to the north-east will be unfit for battle…"

"Meaning if a battle breaks out, we don't expect much fighting from there," Arimnestos finished.

"Hopefully it won't," said Miltiades. "Remember, the plan is to delay for as long as possible until the

Spartans arrive. If we manage to dig in before the Persians do, then we may stand a chance since they won't risk open battle here either."

"Otherwise, things are looking good," said Callimachus, smiling.

"For now, but I still have concerns, especially of their cavalry. Other than the marshlands, the plains are a suitable place for them."

"Only with a larger force could we counter them," said Stesilaos. "Though, if we have enough time, we may be able to set traps or blockades."

Miltiades shook his head. "Better we fortify our position rather than fortify the battlefield. Besides, I don't want our own men getting caught setting traps when the Persians arrive."

"Sir!" A guard called. "Another scout arrived with news of the Persian fleet."

"Bring him," Miltiades commanded.

The guard returned not long after with a tall, thin man. Hollow eyes sunk into his weary face from a lack of sleep. He looked like Miltiades felt.

"Sir," the scout saluted.

"Report."

"Word from Eretria has arrived that the siege is over. Scouts from the Eretrian coasts confirm sighting the Persians onboarding their troops."

"How many?" Miltiades asked.

"They estimated six hundred ships carrying troops with a number of lesser vessels for supplies and thirty thousand men strong."

Miltiades nodded. "Good work soldier. Return to the camps and get a hot meal before getting some rest. You need it."

"Yes, sir!" saluted the scout before leaving.

"Gentlemen!" Miltiades said, turning to the other generals. "The time has come. The Persians will be on the move from Eretria, I still am sure they will land at Marathon. I expect they will sail come morning and begin landfall late afternoon tomorrow. We need to be there before then. So, I propose we march to Marathon and await them there. If they move on, then so shall we."

Stesilaos shook his head while the others nodded before sighing. "We may as well," he said. "Better be ready there than sitting here arguing about it."

Miltiades smiled. "Then begin preparations to march. We leave at dawn."

They nodded in agreement and left the tent to their respective tribes.

By first light of the next day, the army was already on the move towards Marathon, arriving in the bay just before midday.

Various hills dotted the landscape with wide plains and fields. The great marsh swamped the north-east, cushioned by Mount Drakonera.

Along the road south, they found Mount Agrieliki which Stesilaos recommended to camp. Miltiades had his doubts about it initially, but he could not deny the strategic benefits of fortifying their positions there. From the summit of a hill, the entire bay could be seen in clarity.

Just as they began fortifying their position, Persian ships were spotted sailing around the cape before anchoring in the bay. They made it in time.

"I guess they are planning on landing here," Stesilaos commented.

"And it looks like they haven't noticed us yet," said Callimachus.

"They will soon," Miltiades replied. "First, they will bring their horses and other animals so they can recover from the journey. Then their men. Until then, I want us to minimize our presence until it's too late for them to re-embark."

"Then we best warn our men as they will likely send scouts of their own to survey the land," suggested Themistocles.

Miltiades nodded. "Best we don't start unnecessary skirmishes with them just yet. Callimachus, I want reliable men to keep an eye over their horses. I want to know how many and anytime they move."

The Polemarch smiled. "I know just the men for the job!"

Miltiades nodded. "Well, then gentleman. So, it begins."

Before dark, they finished setting the encampment with stakes and barricades outlining the city of tents. The Persians also managed to begin setting their encampment as small boats went back and forth from the floating mass of sails and wood.

Scouts left the Persian camp while soldiers patrolled around it. Miltiades watched them and waited. When Callimachus' scouts returned with their report, Miltiades stood in stunned silence.

*With such a large host, I expected they would bring at least three thousand horses*, he thought. *But a thousand? Something is not right.*

Why did they bring so few? Surely, they knew how important the animals were, so why? Were they *that* arrogant?

Miltiades continued to watch the boats travel to and from shore.

*Wait.*

With only six hundred ships with a number of smaller vessels. Too few to carry such a large host, and horses, and supplies.

*They would have to sacrifice one of these three to make the journey across the Aegean…If so, then they would want to raid small towns and villages.*

The more he thought about it, the more things became clearer for Miltiades. Landing at Marathon was the only choice the Persians truly had if they never brought enough horses. Now with the Athenians here, the Persians could no longer rely on this plan.

Miltiades smiled. *We lucked out then. But those horses will still pose a danger. Best to watch and wait.*

He looked up to the moon in the night sky, getting closer and closer to fullness.

*Soon. It will all be over…Soon.*

\*\*\*

Six days passed since Artaphernes landed at Marathon. Until then, everything went according to plan. The siege of Eretria ended with a few days of fighting when Hippias convinced them to surrender.

Afterwards, they resupplied and sent captives to the small island, Aegilia, to await the army before returning to Persia—as commanded by Darius.

From Marathon, Artaphernes planned on marching to Athens while Datis sailed around the coast to blockade the city and allow Hippias to sway the defenders to surrender.

Now that plan turned to dust and scattered across the winds. Instead of finding an empty bay with a clear path ahead, they found the Athenian army waiting for them, fortified on the base of a mountain, blocking travel on the southern road.

Artaphernes stood over maps brought from Suza, pondering their next move.

"We can't just sit here any longer," argued Hippias, rubbing his jaw. Apparently, he lost a tooth during the landing. "The Spartans will be here soon, and we'll be slaughtered."

"And if we order a retreat back onto the ships now, after committing most of our forces to shore, we will guarantee another disaster," said Datis.

"If we don't do anything now, it's going to turn into one anyway!" yelled Hippias.

"Then what do you propose, Hippias, that we go into battle? Here? With large marshlands on our left flank, ready to swallow any man or horse who dares near it?"

"The marshlands may be unsuited for battle, but the rest of the plains are. The Athenians will also be wary of fighting in that cesspool, so we don't need to worry about being flanked there."

"Even so," said Artaphernes. "We cannot risk open battle, not yet. We still have too few cavalry to work with and the Athenians will overrun our infantry without them."

"Well, we can't go and get them now, can we?" Hippias asked. "The Athenians block the road south and they will attack us if we use the northern road instead. Which I would recommend against anyway since the terrain there is too terrible to march an army into."

"We need horses!" yelled Artaphernes. "At least another thousand. If we have them, then even if the Spartans arrive, we can crush them. We win here, there will be no army left to defend Athens, and to win we need our cavalry."

The tent stood in silence.

"What do you propose then?" the admiral asked.

"The northern road is still open to us, not for the entire army, but at least a small battalion. We would need to send the cavalry we do have. Else it will be too late."

"Most villages north of here would be abandoned, leaving us to send them deep into Thessaly," said Hippias.

"It would also leave us even more vulnerable," said Datis.

"What other option is there? To stay here, do nothing and let the Athenians wait for the Spartans before they attack!? No. The only way we win is to get what we lack."

Datis sighed. "Since time is of the essence, I recommend sending Captain Tithaeus. He may be young, but he is the best cavalry officer I know."

Artaphernes nodded before turning to a messenger. "Then give them the command. Captain Tithaeus and his men are to scour the northern villages as quickly and stealthily as they can. We don't want the Athenians to know we don't have any cavalry."

"Yes, sir!" The messenger saluted before leaving.

"Hopefully this gamble pays off," said Datis.

"You and I both," Hippias agreed.

Artaphernes sighed. "Alright, gentlemen. I believe this concludes our meeting here."

Datis and Hippias nodded before leaving Artaphernes over his maps. The plan had to work. It must.

Artaphernes glanced over the parchment, to the solid lines of Lydia's coasts and the dot where Sardis was. He wondered what his people would be doing— probably enjoying dinner with their families.

He sighed again, wishing the battles were won, and they could sail home.

*It won't be too long from now... I hope.*

\*\*\*

Callimachus went on his early morning patrol around the camp, checking on his men and enjoying the fresh air. He loved it. He never understood why people remained indoors at this time, they never knew what they were missing.

One of his men approached, slowly. The injury on his knee from the march up the mountains had healed, but still troubled him.

"Good morning, Polemarch," he saluted.

"Morning! I see the swelling has gone down!"

"Yes, sir! I'm able to walk, although it still hurts when I try to run. I do pray it heals soon for me to join the battle."

"In time! It will be good to fight alongside you!"

"You honour me, sir!"

Callimachus smiled, patting the soldier's back when another soldier ran to him.

"Polemarch!" he cried.

"Soldier?"

"I bring a report! About the Persian cavalry."

Callimachus' eyes widened as he listened. "Good work, soldier. Return to your post and continue to watch. I need to see our commanding general."

The man saluted and left while Callimachus jogged to the command tent. Miltiades hardly left it since they arrived at Marathon, always going over maps and arguing with himself.

As he thought, the Polemarch found him doing so.

"Good morning, Callimachus. What brings you?" asked Miltiades.

"Morning. I've just received a report from the men watching the Persian cavalry."

Miltiades shot up from the table. "Tell me."

"My men report that the Persians have sent their cavalry up the northern roads. They believe they are going up to Thessaly."

Miltiades raised an eyebrow. "All one thousand?"

"Most of them."

Miltiades pondered for a moment. "Why Thessaly? They can't be searching for a way around, that road is too risky. If it's most of their cavalry, then…" Miltiades smiled.

"Then?"

"Hippias must know the Spartans will be here any day now. They're getting desperate. They've sent men to scour any villages they can up north to bring back horses they lack."

Callimachus nodded. "Then what shall we do about it?"

"We call in the others. It's time we go on the offensive."

Callimachus smiled.

Shortly after, all the generals gathered around a map of Marathon Bay with wooden pieces representing both armies.

"Gentlemen!" Miltiades began. "The time has come to act and end this. The enemy has sent their cavalry north and are vulnerable. They know the Spartans will arrive soon. I propose we attack."

"Then you have a plan?" asked Themistocles.

"Simple. We split our forces into the three flanks and make our lines as long as theirs."

"And be overrun," said Stesilaos. "They still outnumber us. Would it not be wiser to wait for the Spartans before we commit to battle as we intended?"

"We could, but that would give the Persians time to mend their weakened position for a stronger one," said Cynaegirus.

"Alright, then how do you propose we counter their numbers?" asked Stesilaos.

"By having our left and right flanks be eight ranks deep with the centre at four," Miltiades answered. "The men at the centre will need to hold the line long enough for the flanks to encircle the enemy."

"And who will take command of each front?" Arimnestos asked.

"Callimachus will take command of the right wing while you, Commander, will take the left. I'll lead from the centre with Themistocles and Aristides," said Miltiades.

"And what do we do about their archers?" Aristides asked. "It's no good attacking if we get pinned by a rain of arrows."

The Polemarch smiled. "I may have a solution to that, one found in my years of battle! I propose we run once we reach two hundred paces and then sprint at one hundred paces away."

"Like a charging bull," said Themistocles.

"This could work," said Aristides. "If we're fast enough, they won't have a chance to fire more than two volleys."

"I like it," said Miltiades, smiling. "I'll give the commands when we run and sprint." He looked to the generals. "Gentlemen, give the order. This battle should be over before noon. One way or another."

Callimachus smiled even more broadly. "And may Athena bless us with victory!"

# CHAPTER 8

First light rose on the seventh day since Artaphernes had arrived at Marathon. He remained pondering over the maps when a guard entered.

"My lord!" he said in gasping breaths.

"What is it?"

"The Athenians, sir! They're attacking!"

Artaphernes scrambled out of his tent into the ensuing chaos engulfing the camp. He gazed up the hill where the Athenian camp should be, instead finding an army lining their columns.

*It's too soon!* Artaphernes thought. *The Spartans haven't arrived yet. I would have known otherwise!*

"It seems the Athenians couldn't wait any longer," said Datis, exiting his tent already suited in armour. "Especially now since we have no cavalry."

"Then we best get them back," said Artaphernes, turning to a messenger. "Send word to Captain Tithaues and bring them back immediately. *Go!*"

"Yes sir!" The messenger saluted before disappearing.

"And find the other captains. Give them the order to prepare for battle."

"Immediately sir!"

Artaphernes turned back to Datis. "Admiral. I leave command of our centre to you. I'll direct our men from the rear. We must not let the Athenians near our ships else we'll be trapped here."

Datis saluted, barking commands to nearby soldiers running frantically as he left.

Artaphernes went back into his tent, rummaging for all his war gear.

*Damn it all! And we were so close too!* He thought, turning to his father's armour propped on its post.

*I guess it's time.*

\*\*\*

Miltiades watched disarray descend into the Persian camp, however he knew it wouldn't last long. The Athenians' sudden shift to offense may have caught them off guard, but soon their commanders would take charge and prepare for battle. From his experience, the first line were always archers from Ethiopia followed by the infantry.

*This time another surprise awaits them*, he thought, looking to his lines.

"Men! March!"

\*\*\*

"Men! To the centre! Archers to the front!" Datis commanded, as the Ethiopian archers took position. Once the Athenians were in range, a hail of arrow fire would rain on them.

The admiral looked up to the army marching down the mountain.

"Archers!" he called. "Knock your arrows!"

The Athenians marched closer…closer…closer…
"Draw!"
Closer…closer…closer…Now!
"*Loose!*"

Arrows flew into the sky, a dark cloud of death shortly returning down onto the marching Athenians, some hitting their mark, others deflected off their armour and the bronze wall of their shields.

"Nock!...Draw!..."

\*\*\*

"*AT THE—M!*" Miltiades yelled, breaking into a run as the Athenian forces joined behind, shouting battle cries of their own.

\*\*\*

Datis stared in shock as the Athenians turned into a wave of charging bulls. There was no time left for another volley.

"Spears, forward! Archers, behind!" He commanded, as the two lines swapped in time.

Two waves of men crashed into each other, pulling and pushing, with clashes of sword, spear and shield as the battle raged. Those in the first rank stood little to no chance against the surge, and for a moment, Datis worried they would break through.

Then he noticed it. His forces still outnumbered theirs—greatly.

*Their lines are only four ranks deep to match our length! No Spartans have arrived! They're taking as much of a gamble as us! Time for them to pay the price. We just have to break through.*

"Soldiers! Wedge formation!"

A soldier blew a horn, rallying those around them through the chaos into wedge formation.

"Push! Pierce through!"

The Athenians fought back fiercely, like beasts possessed by some mad spirit, standing ground against such odds. And yet, they—a Persian army of near thirty thousand, outnumbering their foes almost two-to-one—seemed on the back foot!

*We must break through! We must!*

Datis fought, hope fading with every fallen man. Was there no way through the Athenian line?

No…There!

A weakness. The Athenians spread themselves thin—too thin. With every clash, every blow, their lines thinned even more. Soon four ranks turned to three, then three to two.

"Forward! We're almost through!"

"Sir! Sir!" A young soldier cried in terror.

Datis turned back in horror as he watched a giant charge down on them from his army's left flank, cutting men like a hot knife through butter. Callimachus, Polemarch and Athen's greatest warrior came, leading his men to the Persian's rear.

*When did they break through?*

He had been too preoccupied with creating an opening to surround the Athenians, he never noticed they were surrounding him. If he didn't act now, it would be too late and there would be no chance for retreat.

"Soldiers! Fall back! Fall back! Protect the rear!"

*We can regroup later, but for now, we must deal with the threat at hand...*

*We could really have used that cavalry about now.*

***

Callimachus fought with all the ferocity he could muster, piercing through the Persians like a spear. So far, Miltiades' plan worked, and they were now surrounding the Persians.

He fought on, leaping across bodies of fallen men, cutting down others as he pushed through towards the Persian rear.

In the distance, he saw Datis, Admiral of the Persian fleet, leading a retreat back to guard against his advance. If the admiral managed to reinforce the rear, it would give them an opportunity to regroup.

*Not on my watch!* Callimachus smiled.

"MEN! WITH ME!"

He charged into the Persian forces, those with enough courage following, his eyes set on his target.

*Not on my watch!*

***

"Sir! Sir! Callimachus is coming this way!"

Datis turned back to where the giant was, darting straight toward him, and cutting down any opposition.

"Form ranks!" The Admiral cried, readying himself for the impact.

Callimachus crashed into his men like thunder, before thrusting his spear at Datis. The admiral blocked it and rushed in with precise strikes forcing the giant on the defence, when the Polemarch's sword swung to his head.

*When did he draw it!?*

The sword came down, Datis stepped back, the blade narrowly missing. After a quick breath, Datis moved in for another attack and the two fell into the rhythmic dance of death, engaged in a flurry of blows, trying to outdo each other—fighting with everything they had.

But Datis knew he was being overwhelmed by pure brutal strength. A heavy blow on his helm sent the admiral back, his ears ringing as blood poured from his wounds, his head feeling light.

Had he lost? When did he fall to the ground? Where was he? What was happening and why was he here?

Men yelled and screamed before joining him in the cold mud. Looking up, a giant covered in bronze roared in triumph, about to plunge his blade, when a spear glided through the air and pierced the giant's throat.

Senses slowly returned to Datis as he watched Callimachus fall, the Athenians around them stood in shock.

Datis felt himself being carried away by his men, retreating from the Athenian beasts who composed themselves and charged with unyielding savagery.

Everything faded to black as he lost consciousness.

***

Damon thrusted his spear, the Persian soldier parried with his shield, leaving an opening for Lydus to finish him. Damon felt glad Lydus was at his side, they made a good team.

Despite the seeming chaotic battle, all Athenians of the central lines worked together pushing the Persians back.

Earlier, he wondered why they were commanded to keep thin ranks until he noticed the Persians delving too deep and news of the Polemarch's advance arrived. He thought it genius, luring the enemy in before swooping in from the sides.

They continued pushing forward.

Although their orders were to hold the line, Damon wanted to go find a worthy opponent when he saw Callimachus lead a charge against the Persians' commander.

Damon smiled. Finally, his opportunity came.

"Hold them!" He told Lydus. "I'll be back now!"

Before Lydus, or anyone, could say a word, Damon rallied his strength and pushed through into the sea of men, yelling, fighting, dodging, until he finally made it to watch the Polemarch's forces clash.

Excitement built within his chest. He would witness a duel only spoken in legends. But he would first need to keep his head to watch it.

He fought and watched, catching glimpses of blows blurring too fast to fully grasp.

The Polemarch overwhelmed the Persian commander, ending with a strike to the head, sending the Persian backwards. The Polemarch roared in triumph. Damon joined in, when horror took him as he watched a spear pierce Callimachus' throat.

Damon remembered Timon's words, "The battlefield is never fair. One-on-one duels without interference only occur in legend."

"NOOOOO!" he yelled, charging into the fray, searching for the cowardly bastard who threw the spear.

There! A Persian directly in line from the two combatants stood with no spear and an outreached arm as if he'd just thrown it.

Damon jumped forward, throwing his spear, getting the Persian in the leg when a shield knocked Damon back and a spear came at him. Out of nowhere, his father pushed Damon aside and took the blow instead.

When did he get here? How did he know where he was? Did Lydus tell him or was the old man watching over him the whole time?

He recalled his father's advice and guilt tore him. If he hadn't been so rash, so reckless, so stupid!

Another spear came towards both of them, miraculously blocked by Lydus and Xenophon.

"Damon!? Damon!? Get up!"

He couldn't answer. Only stare at the blood pouring from his father's chest as Ariston carried him.

More Persians flooded in. Lydus picked Damon up while Xenophon held them back with strength rivalling Callimachus'.

Damon watched as men fought around the dead Polemarch and the defeated Persian commander.

All emotions and eagerness Damon felt days prior to the battle, and even during, died. Replaced by endless guilt and shame.

It was his fault.

*** 

The battle raged on all fronts. Artaphernes watched as thousands of Persian troops lay dead, more being wounded as the mayhem continued.

"Sir! Admiral Datis has been severely injured! He's been carried off back to camp!"

The situation became more hopeless with each passing moment. The Athenians had the upper-hand and if they managed to get to the ships and destroy them...

*No. I won't allow it. I will not be stranded here with no way home!*

"Sir! Captain Tithaues has returned with the cavalry!"

*Too late!*

"What do we do, sir!?"

Artaphernes sighed. "Sound the retreat! Call all men to begin boarding the ships at once! Do not let the Athenians near them!"

"Sir!" Another soldier came running. "The Athenians have captured two of our ships!"

Damn it!

"We need to move! *Now*!" He commanded. The horns sounded as they pulled back. Hopefully they would make it this time.

*What an absolute disaster!*

Mayhem consumed the shores, turning into a slaughter as Persian troops attempted to flee while the Athenian army pursued—led by Cynaegirus and Stesilaos, who had captured seven ships already. Miltiades watched, knowing victory was theirs.

"Give the command to Pheidippides. Let him return to Athens with the news. We have won!"

Themistocles approached, blood stained across his armour. "The Persians have begun setting sail."

"And Athens will be safe."

"For now." The Leontis general stared at the ships pulling away from the shores.

"We should let the Persians go," said Aristides, who had just arrived. "A dangerous animal is a wounded one with nowhere to flee."

Miltiades nodded. "Then call our men back. The day is won. Let there be no need for further bloodshed."

"We should also see to the wounded," said Aristides.

"Well, the Persians won't have any need for their tents and gear," Themistocles added, looking to the abandoned camp.

"Then see it done," said Miltiades. From what he could see, most of his men only suffered minor injuries—some with more serious wounds.

*A bloody miracle…We'll also need a count of the dead.*

As the last Persian ships sailed away, an officer returned. "Sir! I bring tidings from the battle! The other generals have triumphed and are finishing the remnants, but…"

"But what soldier?" Miltiades asked.

"Many have fallen today. Among them are Callimachus, the Polemarch…along with General Cynaegirus and General Stesilaos."

Miltiades stood in shock. He knew of Callimachus, watching the Polemarch during the battle as he duelled Datis, but Cynaegirus and Stesilaos were only at the Persian ships a moment ago.

"What happened to the two generals?"

"Sir! They fell during their attempts to capture the enemies' vessels. Word is spreading that General Cynaegirus even held one at bay with his bare hands before…."

Miltiades sighed. "They were heroes to be remembered. Themistocles. Can I leave you to look after their tribes until a new general is appointed? Themistocles?"

"Apologies, I will. It's just that…It is odd."

"What is?"

"The Persians. I've only seen a small number sail back east while the rest appear to be heading south."

Miltiades watched in silence and swore. Themistocles was right.

"They're going to try and attack Athens while we're stuck here recovering from a battle."

Miltiades swore again. "We need to return immediately. Pheidippides has already been sent back to deliver news of our victory. None will flee by the time the Persians arrive."

"Then it's best we call an emergency meeting with the generals."

"Agreed. Soldier! Send word to the men to rest for now but call the other generals!"

"At once!" The soldier saluted, darting off into the field below.

Moments later, the remaining generals gathered. The absence of the fallen three was felt.

"Gentlemen," Miltiades began. "We may have won this battle, but Athens is still in danger. The Persians have been sighted sailing around the peninsula towards Phaleron."

"Bloody cowards," commented one of the younger generals.

"We have two choices. Either send word back to Athens to warn them, or for us all to run back and hope we make it before the Persians."

"If we send another messenger now," said Aristides, "it will cause confusion as it contradicts the message Pheidippides carries. Some may not flee at all."

"But it could save many more," argued Themistocles. "Right now, our men are exhausted from fighting, and it will be noon soon. Already the sun is too hot. Any run back from here will strain our men and even if we get back in time, I worry about their battle prowess then."

"Themistocles is right," said Miltiades. "And so is Aristides. I am also sure we can reach Athens by late afternoon and still have time to organize ourselves, even on the longer route. I vote to run back."

They all nodded their heads, breathing heavily.

"Then may I make a suggestion?" asked Arimnestos. "Men tend to run quicker with less weight on their backs. I propose we cart down their equipment, marking them and the carts for finding them again."

"We?" Miltiades smiled. "Does that mean Plataea is willing to run back with us?"

"Why not? We came to fight a war, and last I checked, one battle does not constitute as such. Besides, why would I miss out on the victory celebrations?"

They all smiled, nodding.

"Then we shall take the longer route as the shorter is too perilous. The carts must leave first with as many veterans as they can carry," said Miltiades.

"Also," Aristides added, "those unable to run should remain behind and tend to the wounded and dead. We can always return later to clean up the battlefield."

Themistocles nodded. "And those traveling by cart should also warn the villages along the way that the army will be coming through, to prepare water and other aid."

"Very well then," said Miltiades. "We know what must be done. Return to your men and give the order. We move as soon as possible. Themistocles, I leave you to notify the fallen general's tribes. Gentlemen. I shall see you back in Athens and may the gods send us their speed."

They left for their respective destinations while Miltiades stared at the sky as he went to his.

*I'm certain once the Persians see us there, they won't beach, we must just get there in time.*

# CHAPTER 9

Pheidippides ran, slower than usual with his left leg throbbing in pain. He felt it on his run back from Sparta, but after resting, it didn't bother him, until after the battle.

Nevertheless, he needed to return to Athens and deliver the good news. By some miracle or divine intervention, they managed to defeat the Persians without Sparta's aid.

He smiled to himself, recalling his meeting with the two Spartan kings: Leotychidas, elected a year earlier, and Leonidas, who recently succeeded Cleomenes.

They initially impressed Pheidippides with promises of support. Apparently, Cleomenes expected an attack from Persia sooner or later and warned both successors to prepare. Leonidas had been most vocal and keen, promising to personally lead the Spartan army. However, they needed to observe some religious protocols first, but assured they would march immediately after.

*Now we get to impress them with such a victory*! He thought.

His smile broadened along with his pace, still keeping steady to not provoke his injury further. Yet even that proved difficult from the rough terrain of Mount Pentelikos. At times he regretted choosing the shorter route, but he kept reminding himself with every step he neared the garrison at Cephisia.

He just needed to reach their garrison since it was closest to the route and Athens, only being some distance outside the city.

Eventually, he arrived at the foot of Mount Pentelikos, taking a short break, drinking some water, before tackling the treacherous path up the mountain as pain pierced his leg.

*This is going to be a difficult run.*

\*\*\*

Miltiades watched the wagons leave, accompanied by many riders atop horses left behind by the Persians, all carrying veterans eager to return to battle despite their injuries. Aristides left with them to begin defence preparations at Piraeus by the banks of the Illyus River near the sea. He felt confident they would arrive before the Persians.

He reared his horse to turn to the mass of soldiers gathering behind him, preparing for their run back. Themistocles led the rear to look after stragglers while Miltiades led the young and healthy at the front.

"Men of Athens! We run now! Back to our city for her defence! I plead to you all! Run! Run with all your strength! All your might! All the speed you can muster! Run to protect your families! Your home! And may the gods bless us with haste!"

Cheers erupted through the ranks as they ran; a river of men pouring down the long road south to Athens.

\*\*\*

Damon and Lydus ran side-by-side at the army's front. Both eager to return and repel the Persians once more, for good this time. All the running during their training no longer seemed to have been for nothing. Now, after a little rest from the battle, they both felt energized and ready.

Although he mostly focused on running without interrupting the others, Damon couldn't stop thinking about the battle and what occurred. Guilt kept surging in his chest, hollowing it out. If not for his stupidity, his father might be beside them, running with them.

Would his father even survive the injury? What would happen to the family? The farm? Could Damon be able to run it by himself? Would he have to sell it? If he did, what would he do? Why couldn't he have just listened for once!? To heed his father's lessons? About the farm and the battle!

Guilt continued to torment him as he thought. Last he saw the old man was in the infirmary where Ariston stepped up to take care of him. Lydus kept assuring his father knew what he was doing, and Damon's father would be fine. Yet the guilt and worry still tore at him.

He prayed. To the gods, to anyone willing to listen. To spare his father from his injury. To spare himself from these feelings tearing him apart. But to no avail.

It was his fault. He was responsible for it. He would carry this guilt for the rest of his life, knowing he caused his father's death.

And for what!? Glory!? Fame!? Recognition!? Respect!?

Why would anyone praise the deeds of a monster who killed his father and desiccated his legacy!? One who destroyed his family!? Why would anyone respect a child that ignored everything yet still demanded attention!?

Fool! Selfish child! Coward! He was a coward. A coward that hid behind boisterous claims. A coward who lazed around drinking all day, running away from responsibility and reality.

*Truly, at heart, I am a coward. It's time I recognized it and did better. Else father's ghost will haunt me for all time. Whatever may come, I promise to be the man father wanted me to be. I swear on it! Just please, let him live!*

He gave one last prayer for his father before picking up his pace. His father spent years keeping the family together, now he would do the same.

Lydus running next to him was also deep in thought and Damon knew they shared similar concerns. Would they make it in time? Or would they arrive in a city engulfed in flames? Will there be another battle and could they win it all over again on their own?

His thoughts halted when he saw a large group of people in the distance engaged in some activity; still too far to see what. To his knowledge, they should be nearing the first few villages. Was this one of them?

Coming closer, he saw what they were doing. People from the surrounding villages gathered, setting tables on the roadside with pitches, flasks, skins and buckets of water, some with baskets of fruit.

It was a welcoming sight. Thus far the run drained them of the energy brought by determination, but that wouldn't be enough to see them all the way through.

Both Damon and Lydus stopped, pouring cold water over their sweaty faces, sipping between heavy breaths, before joining the run again.

Villagers cried out encouraging praises, congratulating them for their efforts and victory.

*\*\*\**

*That's what they needed*, Miltiades thought. *Something to encourage the warriors.*

He already saw his men running with more vigour and determination to succeed.

*\*\*\**

Somehow, the water break made Damon feel more confident and revitalized. He ran with newfound strength he never knew he had. Not just in body, but in spirit too.

All negative thoughts plaguing him earlier dissipated into the rhythmic motion of his run.

Left foot. Right foot left foot.

He realized even the unclear feelings to Xenophon became clearer. Since risking his life to save Damon and his father, Damon felt indebted to him, now seeing him as a brave warrior and a true friend.

*He would make Hermione happy, much more than I.* He sighed. *Now then. Let's get back and repel those Persians for good and get on with our lives in peace.*

Damon increased his pace, running faster. Those around him did so as well. They were all eager to get home before the Persians.

*Well, they will be in for a shocking surprise,* Damon thought.

*I'll make sure of it!*

\*\*\*

Pheidippides continued to climb, making good progress despite his injured leg. He made sure to take cautious steps along the rough road, to not lose his balance or step on a loose rock.

He couldn't wait to see the people's faces when he announced the victory. In anticipation, he increased his strides, climbing faster when a sharp pain pierced his leg as he stood on a stone. The stone loosened and he fell, hitting his head on a rock before everything turned to black.

Moments later, he woke, his senses fled with his head in a haze. His skull pounded, sweat covering his face. He searched for his face cloth, wiping his forehead, his eyes widening when he saw red.

His face burned like it was aflame. Quickly, he poured water over where he felt the wound, tore a piece off his tunic and tightly wrapped it around his head. He sat on the ground, breathing heavily, trying to gather his strength.

Somehow, he needed to deliver the message. The garrison wasn't far, but he was still a way off. He slowly stood, his feet staggering, forcing his knees to stop shaking.

The hot midday sun made his ordeal more difficult, and he wished for some cloud cover.

*I must complete my task,* he thought as blood ran down his face.

*No matter what.*

\*\*\*

Theodorus watched his surroundings, gazing down the top of Mount Pentelikos and into the valley of cypress trees and small bushes below. Since the army passed through a few days' prior, the guard station had been quiet. By now, they would be battling the Persians in Marathon.

*Cousin's fighting a war, and what do I get? Guard duty!* He thought bitterly. Yet here he stood with the garrison in case any messengers came this way.

Noon passed when he spotted a distant figure moving towards them in awkward motions.

"Philon!" he called the guard beside him, pointing to the figure. "What do you make of that?"

"A messenger maybe? From his movements, he seems injured. See to him while I call the others."

Theodorus nodded, hiking down the path. Coming closer, he recognized the figure behind the blood-soaked cloth around his head.

"Pheidippides!?" He cried. "What happened!?"

"Vic…Vict…" Pheidippides stuttered before falling on his knees.

Theodorus rushed to the messenger and tried to help him to his feet, but Pheidippides did not move. Instead, he reached a handout from his torn blood-stained tunic and pulled the guard down.

"Victory," he whispered. "We…we won…We…won…" His grip loosened as Philon and the others arrived with their captain.

Theodorus looked up, tears welling in his eyes. "He's gone."

"Did he say anything?" the captain asked.

"Yes. We won. They managed to defeat the Persians."

The men looked at each other in silence.

"Alright then," said the captain. "Let's regroup. Send word to Athens with the news. Let all know Pheidippides died carrying his last message of victory. We all owe this man for his devotion."

They nodded.

"Now, help me bring his body to camp. We need to make arrangements to send him back to Athens for a proper burial."

"Yes sir!" They saluted, gently picking up the messenger's body.

Theodorus watched in silence.

*He truly was a hero to the people of Athens.*

# CHAPTER 10

Artaphernes stood on his flagship's deck surrounded by the captains and Hippias as they passed the Cape of Sounion. In the distance, fire lit atop a watchtower then another further away.

"They know we are coming," said Hippias. "Athens will be warned before we arrive at Phaleron."

"And see what forces remain to defend it," a captain said confidently, despite their previous failure.

"I doubt there will be many since their army is in Marathon," said another.

Artaphernes shook his head, walking away and leaned over the railing to watch the waves crash upon the rocky shores. He felt sick and his stomach heaved with the waves.

No matter how hard he tried focusing on planning, his mind kept lingering on the events at Marathon. They clearly underestimated the Athenians, their timing of the assault and their tenacity...nobody expected it.

*If only I acted sooner,* he thought. *Or even if I sent scouts to shore before committing the army, then maybe...if only Datis was here.*

Artaphernes missed the admiral, who always brought sound advice. However, due to his injuries, Artaphernes ordered him to return home with the other wounded, collecting the Eretrian prisoners along the way.

*If only…*

Thinking about doing things differently was pointless now. Without the admiral's input, he needed to make the right call, otherwise all would be lost.

Artaphernes sighed thinking of Sardis, wishing not for the thousandth time he was home instead of being stuck warring in a foreign land.

Despite the captains' claims, he knew they sailed to an unknown fate—except for what Hippias told them of the terrain. The rocky coastlines of Piraeus prevented vessels from beaching leaving only the harbour to go ashore, providing the city remained undefended.

Troop morale also worried him, knowing their loss weighed heavily on their minds; even on the minds of the captains who were trying to rectify it.

Hippias startled Artaphernes, joining him alongside the rail. Both watched the waves lapping the shores in silence. The exiled tyrant sighed when they passed a small fishing hut.

"I used to visit here in Sounion with my family when I still ruled Athens. Often the local farmers and fishermen invited us as guests; how they smiled to be my host…" He sighed again, shaking his head. "Now I return as their enemy. To take their homes and families… Do you know how sickening that is? To watch all your friends and family; all those who once loved and praised you, turn their backs, wanting nothing more to do with you?"

Artaphernes answered with silence.

"If we lose here and now..." Hippias continued, tears welling in his eyes. "...should I be captured...they'll execute me for sure."

Pity. Pity was all Artaphernes felt for this man. After first meeting him in Suza, he initially felt disgusted by one who would eagerly betray his people and sell them to retain some semblance of power, which was still true. Except now, all that stood before Artaphernes was a broken, twisted, and desperate man trying to hold onto everything dear to him as it slips through his fingers. Someone longing to return home.

A strong southern wind blew, pushing the Persian ships faster. Artaphernes placed a hand on Hippias' back.

"We'll reach Piraeus before dark," he said to Hippias. "You work your magic like back in Eretria and hopefully the city surrenders before more reinforcements arrive."

"I wonder about that," said Hippias.

Artaphernes turned back to the captains. "Gentlemen. Return to your vessels and prepare your men. We'll attack on my command under the cover of night."

"Yes sir!" The captains saluted before leaving. One way or another, it would all end.

Dusk came when the fleet circled the final cape before Athens, only to be greeted with the worst possible sight they could ever imagine. Athenian soldiers lined the shores of Phaleron, standing firm in battle formation while archers eyed them from the hillsides. Ahead, six Athenian ships blocked the harbour's entrance. Artaphernes took another gamble, and it failed…again.

"Men! Withdraw! Withdraw!" He yelled. "With haste!"

Their ships drew back towards the islands of Salamis and Aegina, hopefully to buy them time.

"Call for the captains!" he ordered.

Artaphernes stood, puzzled. Where did these soldiers come from? Were they another army? Surely not! Otherwise, they would have been at Marathon. The Athenians couldn't afford to split their forces. Then could they be the same army from Marathon? If so, how did they manage to get here so quickly?

Once again, the Athenians timing and tenacity was impeccable knowing no bounds.

*Would I too not go through such endeavours and hardship to protect my home?* He thought to himself. *Whatever the case may be, they're waiting for my decision.* To attack or to retreat.

Hippias and the captains returned to their flagships.

"Gentlemen," Artaphernes began. "We are in dire straits and attacking now would be too reckless. Our men will be easy pickings for those archers. Also, our ships will be in range for them to throw oil or other flammables to destroy them. And attacking the harbour will be inadvisable since their ships are in position. Even if we manage, any sunken ship will block us anyway."

"On top of that," Hippias added, "it's the third night of the full moon. The Spartan's can't be too far off. Even if we win the battle tonight, we'll lose it tomorrow. And if Corinth joins or Argos? We'll be trapped."

"And there's also the possibility of Aegina changing sides since we are on the back foot," said Artaphernes. "They may be allies for now, but they too are Greeks and our presence threatens them. We cannot afford a prolonged campaign, and we cannot suffer a second defeat."

"Then what do you propose, General?" A captain asked.

Artaphernes sighed. "The only thing we can…"

*\*\*\**

Miltiades watched the fleet from shore, the full moon lighting the sea allowing them to observe the Persians, ready to give the command should they attack. They were all ready for another battle.

Aristides led archers, equipped with Persian bows left behind at Marathon, to the hilltops while Themistocles waited eagerly aboard one of the six ships, knowing his smaller vessels were faster and more mobile in the narrow Salonic bay.

It did not surprise Miltiades when the Persians immediately retreated away from Phaleron after arriving.

*Honestly, I would have done the same*, he thought.

Their soldiers would be demoralized and exhausted from fighting a losing battle, only to sail around Sounion just to fight another difficult battle. No general, even those of brilliant minds, would risk it, unless their men rested first.

All while the Athenians returned with ample time to rest and prepare, the only fires coming from the watchtowers. Miltiades felt grateful to have led such determined men who pushed and fought with such great effort. If it were not for them, Athens would have already fallen.

After spending more time observing the Persians, Miltiades concluded they would not attack until their soldiers rested.

Our men should do the same.

"Send word to Themistocles and Aristides. They are to rest their men and leave a few sentries to watch the Persians."

"Yes sir!"

Miltiades knew the invaders only had two realistic choices. Attack or leave.

*Either way, it comes to an end.* He sighed, deciding to join his men for a much-needed rest.

They earned it.

\*\*\*

Damon and Lydus stood in formation, spear and shield readied, guarding the harbour entrance from the land. Relief came when they received the command to rest until further notice.

They smiled at each other and gathered with their companions sharing food rations around the fire, keeping them warm against the cold autumn sea breeze.

"Is there going to be another battle?" Lydus asked.

One of the veterans smiled, shaking his head. "I may not be a general, but in my experience, those with a clear head tend to retreat for a better position. They're tired, demoralized, and have no foothold to lead a successful landing."

"Charylaos is right," said another veteran. "Even if they attempted landing somewhere else, the underwater reefs would damage their ships and leave them stranded; and they know that. Besides, we hold strong positions here, so don't worry. Sooner or later, we'll all be back home."

"I'd rather be there sooner than later," complained Lydus. "I have a family to take care of."

"We all do," Charylaos laughed, others joining him.

Damon sat silently, staring into the fire as thoughts of his father and family flashing into his mind as guilt crept in. He may have decided to be a better man, promising to live up to his father's expectations, but he still didn't know if he could. You simply don't change overnight.

*I'll at least take those first steps*, he thought. *I can do that much.*

"Are you alright?" Lydus asked, placing a hand on Damon's shoulder.

"I just hope father pulls through."

"I'm sure he will. He's a tough old goat, especially since he constantly deals with you."

"Rich coming from a son who nearly destroyed his father's vineyard from a horse race."

"Now that's unfair! It only happened because you kept boasting about how good you were and then cheated in that race!"

"...Sorry."

"...Damon...Listen...What happened wasn't your fault..."

"But it was! If I hadn't left my post to be a hero, father would still be here."

"You can't know that for sure. Remember what Timon said, 'anything can happen in a battle.'"

"Still. It *did* happen, because of *me*!" Damon sighed. "...All I can do now is make amends."

They sat in silence when Charylaos spoke. "Damon. Some advice from an elder here. We've all been young and stupid with ideas of heroism and glory; even your father. No one is able to live long without making a mistake or two. What is important isn't the mistake, but learning from it and making sure it never happens again."

"Unlike our Persian guests across the bay," added the other veteran.

Charylaos chuckled. "Yes, not like them...my own father once said, 'If you keep fishing in the same spot every day and catch nothing, you're either in the wrong spot, using the wrong bait or just simply a bad fisherman.'"

Damon smiled, remembering similar sayings from Demetri when he, in his younger years, went in the morning to buy fish. Now his sister went. She also took up every chore Damon neglected while he drank and slept his days away.

Why? What for? To keep drinking into late hours of the night and sleep all morning?

It's time to grow up.

He highly appreciated the veteran's advice, putting his mind at ease.

"Anyway, I think it's time we got some sleep," Charylaos suggested. "It's going to be a long day tomorrow."

"Only if the Persians don't attack us tonight," said Lydus.

"I doubt it."

Damon lay his head down and continued to stare into the flames. His eyes felt heavy, slowly closing while he thought of his father, his family, and his past, until eventually sleep took him.

Darkness surrounded him when Damon awoke to Lydus shaking him.

"The Persians are on the move."

Damon shot up and prepared himself with the others, throwing water onto his face to wash away the sleep. Soon they were back in battle formation.

From his position, Damon could see where the generals were stationed along with the Persian ships in the distance, barely able to see in which direction they were sailing.

"Ready yourselves!" Themistocles' order echoed.

His rowers composed to act as soon as the Persians came closer while archers by Aristides knocked their arrows.

Slowly, the Persian ships sailed to Phaleron, all soldiers tensed, ready. Just before they reached shallow waters, the Persian vessels turned right towards Sounion.

They all stood in surprise when Damon heard Miltiades' cry. "They are leaving!"

A huge relief fell across the entire army as the dread of another battle lifted. The Persians did not beach. No more Athenian blood would be spilt.

Scouts rode south along the cape to observe the fleet. They all knew, until the last Persian ship disappeared from sight at Sounion, anything could still happen. Thus, they stayed composed in silence befitting true professional soldiers.

Noon came when the last Persian vessel disappeared from their view. Only then did Themistocles and his troops return to land while Miltiades' orders came for them to gather for food, rations and water.

Not since the night before the battle a lifetime ago, Damon finally ate a decent hot meal, and never before had cooked rations tasted so good. He looked at Mount Pentelikos, to Marathon.

*Looks like things will turn out fine, after all.*

\*\*\*

Once he finished his meal, Miltiades called the other generals to discuss further plans to bring the wounded back from Marathon and bury the dead. According to his scout's reports, although they suffered around two hundred casualties, the Persians lost over six thousand: a remarkable feat. How they managed that with a smaller, vastly outnumbered force, only the gods knew.

Furthermore, since hearing of Pheidippides' death when arriving in the city, he felt the loyal messenger deserved an honourable funeral. He gave much to Athens, including his life. Athens would repay him.

While waiting, the watchtowers lit once more. He watched the Persian ships retreat the night before and sent scouts to Sounion to watch their movements. The signal fires ablaze meant one thing; the Persians were gone for good.

Breathing a sigh of relief, he turned to one of his men. "Let them all know. Victory is ours!"

The soldier saluted and left with a gleeful smile. Soon the whole army erupted in shouts and jeers, raising their weapons to the sky, saluting their generals.

"NENIKIKAMEN!" They yelled. We won!

Cries of laughter and tears echoed across the valley? and amidst the joy and relief, a messenger arrived.

"Sir! The Spartans! They have arrived!"

A wide grin swept across Miltiades' face. He turned to the arriving generals.

"Shall we go meet our guests?"

# CHAPTER 11

Leonidas led his army of two thousand Spartan warriors to the city gates. For three days they marched to Athens' call for aid. When they passed the base of Mount Aigaleo, the city came into view. Neither smoke, fires nor any signs of battle or siege plagued their sight. Relief washed over Leonidas then.

However, upon closer inspection, he noticed activity along the harbour and nearby shores. Athenian ships readied for battle while troops, stationed at various strategic points, waited.

*The Athenians are here, yet no Persian army or fleet is in sight.*

According to his messenger's last report, the Athenians held Marathon, preventing the Persians from progressing while they waited for reinforcements.

*Are we too late? Has Marathon been lost and now they expect battle here?*

"Quick, to the gates," he ordered his men, and they increased their tempo.

As they neared Piraeus, a company on horseback rode to greet them, Miltiades at their front.

"Greetings, King Leonidas!"

"Greetings, General Miltiades! I have brought my men as requested. I hope we aren't too late?"

Miltiades smiled. "I'm afraid so. You see, we've already battled the Persians…and won."

Leonidas looked in disbelief, wondering how an army so outnumbered claimed victory. "Please, tell me how you managed that?"

"In due time. First, let us proceed to a more suited place for talk and let your men rest."

Leonidas nodded, ordering his men to rest before following the Athenian general with his captains to the command centre, where the other generals awaited them. Settling down, the Athenians began to explain the events of what transpired since the last reports. He listened intensely.

It sounded like something out of legends. With Miltiades' concern of the Persian cavalry to their disappearance north. The plans of attack, the charge into battle and the epic clash of Callimachus and Datis. Sorrow filled Leonidas upon hearing of the Archon's fall.

He continued listening about the Persian retreat and the loss of Cynaegirus and Stesilaos, who chased the enemy to their ships. His captains gasped hearing about how Cynaegirus held a ship with his bare hands before losing them to an axe, or so the men who witnessed it claimed.

However, none impressed Leonidas more than the Athenians run back after realising the Persians were sailing to Athens. Such determination to arrive in less than a day and with enough time to prepare…no wonder the Persians retreated. At the tale's end, the Spartan King and his captains had nothing but praise for the Athenians and Plataeans.

"Would you allow us to travel to Marathon and see for ourselves?" Leonidas asked.

Miltiades nodded. "We need to return as well to help our wounded and bury the dead. There are spoils from the Persian camp too, but first our men need to rest. If there are no objections, I vote we depart the day after tomorrow with some volunteers."

"Agreed," said Aristides, "I vote each general provides a hundred men for the task, so that each tribe shares in the burden equally.

"I can also provide five hundred to help," Leonidas offered, and Miltiades nodded in agreement.

"Then it's decided. We'll leave in two days with one and a half thousand while the rest of the army remain behind to recuperate."

With the plans decided, Leonidas joined the rest of his warriors, who began mingling with the Athenians, and told them of his meeting. During the telling, he felt an eager excitement to see the battlefield himself.

*One day, I hope to fight in such a heroic battle*, he thought. *One day...*

***

Damon awoke before the sun rose, although he hardly slept at all. Anxiety and worry ate at him since hearing the commands for men to volunteer returning to Marathon. He had been one of the first to do so.

He needed to know what happened to his father. Was the injury worse than expected? Would he become a cripple? Would he even be alive?

Often these questions plagued him, and every time they did, Lydus and the others would cheer him up, Xenophon too. He appreciated their efforts, else he'd gone mad with worry.

At least the return trip would be by horse and wagon without needing to run or carry equipment. But if it were up to Damon, he would have left already.

Sitting next to ash-covered embers of the dead fire, Damon gazed north-east to the mountains, to Marathon, when Lydus came with breakfast.

"Strange seeing you up so early," his friend teased, handing him a bowl of porridge.

"Not so strange these days."

"I guess…"

The two sat there enjoying the quiet roll of waves and general hubbub of the morning camp.

"Damon!" a sentry called. "There is a visitor here to see you!"

He and Lydus looked at each other, got up and went to see. They followed the sentry to the camp's entrance where Daphne waited. Before a word could be said, she darted to him and hugged so tightly he thought he would lose his breath.

"Alright! Alright! It's good to see you too."

She slightly loosened her grip. "Where is father?"

A knife of guilt pierced Damon's heart. "He's still at Marathon… A spear caught him during the battle and had to remain behind after the battle."

She hugged tighter again, and Damon could hear faint whimpers.

"I wouldn't worry too much," said Lydus. "My father stayed with him to look after his wounds. Besides, it isn't a fatal one."

"One battle and now you're an expert physician!?" Daphne asked him between sobs.

Lydus smiled awkwardly. "Well...no, but both my father and Themistocles agree if the wound were serious, he'd be losing more blood than he did."

"I hope they're right," she whispered, releasing her grip and wiping her red eyes before handing Damon a basket. "Here, for you. I brought one for father too."

Inside, Damon found meat, bread, cheese, fruit and some honey cakes. "I'll take it to him. We leave again tomorrow to bring the wounded home and bury the dead."

She nodded, giving him the second basket.

"By the way, how did you know I'd still be alive, let alone be stationed here?" Damon asked jokingly.

"Intuition. Besides, I can't imagine bull heads like you dying easily. At least that's what mother has been saying since you left...I guess I'll be able to give her some good news then..." She looked at him with her deep brown eyes, puffy red circles around them. "Please bring father home?"

"I will. I promise."

She hugged him once more and Lydus too before swiftly leaving with her companions. They both walked back to their dead fire, sharing the meal from Damon's basket. A home cooked meal was a most welcome gift especially since living on army rations for over two weeks.

They spent the rest of the day packing and preparing. Soon dawn rose again with a convoy of carts and wagons leaving the encampment to the mountains, a battalion of Spartan warriors and their King with them.

Surprisingly, the journey did not take as long as the previous two, or so it seemed to Damon. Yet the closer they got, the greater his anxiety grew, to the point where all he wanted to do was jump off the cart and run ahead.

Eventually they arrived back in Marathon, greeted with cheers by those who remained behind, all eager to return home to their loved ones. Some even managed to dig a burial mound for the fallen Athenians and Plataeans, but the mass number of Persians corpses still littered the fields.

Damon saw the disbelief on the Spartans' faces as they examined the battlefield, amazed the Persians suffered such a devastating defeat. Even their camp was left mostly untouched as they didn't have time to salvage themselves or their ships. Great would be the spoils, yet none of it interested Damon anymore. Only one thing consumed his mind.

As soon as the wagons stopped, he jumped off and dashed to the tents housing the wounded. He almost tripped doing so if not for Lydus catching him. They both rushed in, running to the bed where Damon last saw his father. His knees buckled as his heart skipped a beat. The bed was empty.

Both looked around them, searching for an explanation. Dark thoughts entered Damon's mind with guilt. Maybe his father died and was buried under that mound. Maybe…

Ariston entered. "I thought you both would come here first."

"Where is my father?"

Ariston smiled gently. "Simon is fine. He is outside with the others enjoying the sun. I did say the wound was not serious."

A wave of relief washed away the anxiety and guilt, drowning out the rest of Ariston's words. "Can you take me to him? Please!?"

Ariston nodded. "Come. He is waiting."

Lydus' father led them to an open area where a number of wounded soldiers relaxed under the sun, gazing at the sea. Damon found his father sitting on a rock with his eyes closed. He ran to him, embracing the old man just as Daphne had done with him.

"Oh! Not so tightly!"

"Father! I'm sorry! I'm so sorry! It was my fault! My fault you got hurt! It's all my fault, I'm so sorry!" Tears ran down Damon's cheeks.

"Don't think too highly of yourself that everything happened because of you. Anything could have happened in that battle."

"But if I hadn't…if I had never left my post and tried to be a hero, you wouldn't have needed to come save me!"

"And yet we still live. That's what's most important. So, there is no use torturing yourself over what-if or what-could-have been. What matters is we are still here."

Damon held his father for a few moments before finally letting go. "Will you be able to travel back?"

"Not so soon, I imagine. It will still take some days to clean up. By then, I'll be more than ready. Until then, the only bad thing for me to worry about is the food."

"Ah!" Damon jumped remembering. He ran back to the carts, grabbing the basket before running back and handing it to his father. "From Daphne."

His father smiled while opening it. "Looks like a proper meal came sooner than expected," he laughed. "I'll be sure to thank her."

He divided the food and shared it amongst them before turning to Ariston. "Thank you, my friend, for looking after me. If not for your constant change of my bandages, I'm sure the wound would have worsened."

Ariston shrugged. "Again, your wound was not that bad. Besides, is that not what friends are for? I am sure you would have done the same."

"Whatever the case! I'm just thankful that you helped me pull through."

"You know," Damon said to Lydus while their fathers continued talking, "I hope one day, you and I will have such a bond."

"Don't we already?"

Damon smiled. "I don't think beating each other up counts."

"Well, it was over a girl who played us both for fools."

"Yes…well let's not make that mistake again, shall we?"

"Agreed."

The two shook hands and joined their fathers' conversation, laughing as they told tales of old times from their youths. For a time, Damon wished this moment would never end.

\*\*\*

"Gather the men and begin burying the dead, the ground near the marshlands should be soft enough for trenches. We don't want to risk the spread of disease," Miltiades commanded.

"At once!" The soldier soon left the general to gaze at the blood-soaked bay. Despite commanding the battle himself, he could hardly believe the casualty count when he heard it.

Out of the eleven thousand Greeks that charged into battle, only one hundred and ninety-two fell—the two generals and the Polemarch included. However, the staggering six thousand Persian bodies littering the fields...that was something out of legends.

"After burying the dead, we will also need to move the spoils back to Athens," said Miltiades.

"Those horses and wagons left by the Persians will be a big help there," said Aristides.

"Even then, I suspect we will need a second trip," Themistocles added. "There is much to carry; a large number of sheep, goats and chickens among them."

"Meant to feed the Persian army," Miltiades commented. "There should also be numerous bags of wheat, barley and other cereals."

"Seems the Persians are sponsoring the victory banquet," Themistocles smiled.

"Maybe we should send a 'thank you' to Darius," Aristides jested.

Themistocles chuckled. "Maybe we should."

Miltiades smiled as well and sighed. "We should also send men to gather the rest of the abandoned armour along with other equipment to sustain an army."

"And what of the wounded?" Aristides asked.

"Let us give their injuries time to mend. I want them home within the next two days. Until then, we best salvage as much as we can."

The two nodded and got to work. Bit by bit, Miltiades felt the tension within his muscles loosening. He gazed across the fields of Marathon once more and smiled.

*** 

Damon eagerly welcomed the news of transporting the injured in two days. He wanted to bring his father home where his mother and a physician could mend and look after him.

First, however, was the gruelling job of carrying corpses to the trenches for burial. In the past, Damon would have come up with any excuse to avoid such hard work, but not now. His prayers had been answered and he would keep his promise.

The days passed and with the battlefield cleared, they began the journey home; a painful one for his father, Damon saw. Every bump and nook on the road made his father grimace with pain despite his efforts to hide it.

Eventually, the wagons arrived back in Athens, taking each warrior they carried to their own homes. Soon the familiar roof peaked over the hill as their home came into view, his mother and Daphne waiting by the door.

Together with Lydus and Ariston, they guided his father into the house. Both he and Damon thanked Lydus and Ariston for their aid once again before the two women assisted the old man to his bedchamber. There, he could rest peacefully.

Damon, along with Lydus and Ariston, left for the army camp once again. They could only return after being dismissed once the campaign was declared complete. Damon just felt glad things could finally come to an end.

# CHAPTER 12

The day after returning, Miltiades called the generals and the Spartan king for a final meeting.

"Gentlemen. We come today to end our campaign of defending Athens from Persia. In this, we have found victory against all odds, after winning an astonishing battle. Nevertheless, those fallen must be respected and honoured. Thus, I propose a special tribute for those who gave their lives, and let Athens pay their final respects to these heroes. The messenger Pheidippides especially for his remarkable dedication and loyalty."

"Agreed," said Themistocles. "We should hold a ceremony the day before the victory banquet."

Aristides nodded. "We also need to make plans to deliver welfare to the families of the fallen and especially the young widows with children."

"Very well then," Miltiades said. "Aristides, I shall leave that to you. If there is nothing else...then I hereby conclude this campaign!"

They all broke into their own circles. Miltiades approached the King of Sparta, who talked with his captains about plans for returning.

"King Leonidas. Will you be joining us for the victory feast?"

"I'm afraid not. It is not my victory to celebrate."

"But you and your men are most welcome."

"That is kind of you…but no. We will be leaving after the ceremony."

"Very well," Miltiades nodded in understanding. The king may not have shown it, but to Miltiades, he seemed concerned about not wanting to cause a fuss knowing his own men's frustrations; lest a fight break out.

He sighed. *It may be best this way.*

\*\*\*

Damon and Lydus arrived at their tribe's banquet site with other younger warriors the morning prior to the feast. Instructions came for them to clear and prepare the area. They began offloading the chairs and tables from their wagons while others dug pits for cooking fires.

Daphne arrived in the afternoon, accompanied by other maidens, to help decorate the tables with flowers. When Damon was called somewhere else, leaving Lydus alone to clean and dust chairs, she approached her brother's friend hastily and hugged him.

"What's this all of a sudden?'"

"I just wanted to thank you properly for all you've done. Damon told me how you risked your life to save him and my father."

"To be honest, I was terrified when it happened, but I couldn't just leave them either…"

"Whatever the case. Thank you. I wouldn't mind finding a husband as brave as you one day," she said, and before Lydus could even ask what she meant, another woman called her.

She briskly walked away, giving him a quick glance and smile. He continued to stare in her direction blankly. For as long as he knew her, Lydus only ever saw her as a little sister—like Cassandra. But now…

"What's wrong?" Damon asked, returning.

"Nothing."

Damon looked at him with a raised eyebrow.

"Seriously Damon. I'm fine. Just lost in thought, that's all."

"Right…" said Damon, sounding unconvinced.

"Really, I…"

Sound of hooves echoed through the site, thankfully taking Damon's attention away. They ran to the roadside to find Themistocles with his twenty chosen men returning from the ceremony. Among them was Xenophon.

"You know something," Damon said to his friend. "When I heard of Xenophon's proposal to Hermione, I hated him. But since the battle, I no longer feel that way."

"If it weren't for him, both of us and other fathers would be buried under the mound back at Marathon."

Damon nodded. "He's a true hero…I just don't know how to repay him."

"Well, why don't we just be good friends with him?" Lydus suggested. "Come. Let's go congratulate him for his upcoming wedding."

"Good idea."

They approached the gentle giant, already off his horse.

"Good day Xenophon," Damon greeted. "How was the ceremony?"

"Sad...I can't believe there are so many no longer with us. I feel for their families...especially Ameinias. He's not taking the loss of his brother, General Cynaegirus, well."

"Such is the result of war, I guess," said Lydus and the three stood in silence for a time.

"...Anyway," said Damon. "We just wanted to congratulate you on your wedding."

Xenophon looked at him. "Thanks, but how did you know about it? It was meant to be a secret until after the celebrations."

"Good news travels fast," said Lydus, shrugging his shoulders.

"Besides, I'm sure you and Hermione will make a good couple," Damon added.

"Hermione!?" Xenophon asked in astonishment. "I'm not marrying Hermione, but beautiful and gentle Aspasia–Andromachus' daughter."

Damon and Lydus looked at each other, speechless. After regaining their wits, Damon cleared his throat. "Ah, sorry. We must have misunderstood."

"Yes," Lydus said bashfully. "We heard you were getting married and assumed it was with Hermione since she is always around you."

"She's always around everyone," said Xenophon. "Can't seem to be in one place at any given time... Also, she's friends with my sister."

"Well, anyway, congratulations. Aspasia is a lovely lady," said Damon.

"Of course she is! That's why I proposed to her…listen, let me sort my horse and I'll join you shortly."

Damon and Lydus nodded, leaving him to finish.

"Lydus? Who told you about Xenophon's wedding?"

"Cassandra. You?"

Damon sighed and looked at him. "Daphne."

They both turned to look at their sisters who were busy arranging flowers on a table.

"The vixens," cursed Damon. "We've been set up. I should have known better!"

"Not much we can do about that now?" Lydus chuckled.

"Not until they decide to catch us with another one. I mean how foolish do they think we are?"

"Foolish enough to fall for their tricks."

They both sighed then burst into laughter.

Damon cleared a tear from his eye. "What now?"

"Come. Let's get drunk tonight. You still owe me from the last time we went drinking."

"Why don't we leave that for tomorrow, and not drink too much either. I need to look after the farm while my father recovers."

Lydus nodded. "I understand. I'll probably need to do the same. There is still much I need to learn before taking over."

"They both worked hard enough all their lives for us. Now it's our turn."

"Well said!"

"Themistocles!?" They both jumped around to find the Leontis tribe leader in front of them.

"I came to see how the preparations were going," said Themistocles, looking around.

"So far, so good…sir," said Lydus.

"Sir? If I may?" Damon asked. "I'm just curious as to which tribe will be hosting the Spartans."

"Oh. The Spartans have already left. King Leonidas politely refused, specifying it wasn't their victory. But if you ask me, I think he was just concerned a fight might break out between his men and our own. After a few drinks, even two brothers will turn to enemies over trivialities."

Damon and Lydus chuckled.

"We know that all too well," said Damon rubbing his jaw.

Themistocles smiled at them and walked forward to stare across the bay, towards the silhouette islands of Aegina and Salamis.

Lydus and Damon joined him. Damon looked to the harbour, recalling the night before the Persians left. "Do you think they will try again?"

Themistocles nodded. "They will. They will come back for sure. And when they do, we'll be ready and waiting for them."

# EPILOGUE

Themistocles' prediction would turn out true as the Persians attempted a second invasion of Greece ten years later under Xerxes, Son of Darius, who would succeed his father in taking the Persian throne.

With the army in Themistocles' command and using money from the newly found silver mines around Athens, a strong fleet of over two hundred trireme ships were built.

Later the Persians would win a victory at the Battle of Thermopylae, where the famous last stand of the three hundred Spartans—led by Leonidas—took place alongside their other allies. A heroic stand that was to alter the fate of Europe.

The invaders would then face two crushing defeats: One in the Battle of Salamis against the army led by Themistocles, and again in the Battle of Plataea a year later.

As for Artaphernes, who after returning to Persia with captives from Eretria, would never again partake in any military activity and remain in Lydia for the rest of his days.

The captives, brought before Darius, had impressed the king with their bravery, so that he pardoned them, giving them land in the province of Cissia in exchange for their allegiance.

A hundred and fifty years later the Persians would face their final defeat against an army led by Alexander the Great. This turning point in history would spread Greek civilization, along with values of freedom and democracy, across the known world.

Thus, I wish to commend the Marathon runners alongside the other Greek soldiers, who fought for the preservation of their ideals for the freedom of future generations.

So today I ask, when we watch any long-distance race, to spare a thought for those first runners of Marathon, who ran against so many odds and when so much was at stake

www.ingramcontent.com/pod-product-compliance
Lightning Source LLC
Chambersburg PA
CBHW020752210626
46807CB00018B/2823

* 9 7 8 0 7 9 6 1 9 7 0 3 0 *